T0029616

TOMÁS GONZÁLEZ

Difficult Light

Translated from the Spanish by Andrea Rosenberg

archipelago books

Copyright © Tomás González, 2015
English translation © Andrea Rosenberg, 2020
First Archipelago Books Edition, 2020

All rights reserved. No part of this book may be reproduced or transmitted in any form without
the prior written permission of the publisher.

Library of Congress Cataloging-in-Publication Data:
Names: González, Tomás, 1950- author. | Rosenberg, Andrea, translator.
Title: Difficult light / Tomás González ; translated from the Spanish by Andrea Rosenberg.
Other titles: Luz difícil. English
Description: First Archipelago Books edition. | Brooklyn, NY : Archipelago Books, 2020.
Identifiers: LCCN 2020014356 | ISBN 9781939810601 (paperback) | ISBN 9781939810618 (ebook)
Classification: LCC PQ8180.17.O483 L8913 2020 | DDC 863/.64--dc23
LC record available at https://lccn.loc.gov/2020014356

Archipelago Books
232 3rd Street #A111
Brooklyn, NY 11215
www.archipelagobooks.org

Distributed by Penguin Random House
www.penguinrandomhouse.com

Cover art: Saul Leiter, Perry Street Cat, c. 1949
© Saul Leiter Foundation, courtesy Howard Greenberg Gallery

This work was made possible by the New York State Council on the Arts with the support of
Governor Andrew M. Cuomo and the New York State Legislature. Funding for the translation
of this book was provided by a grant from the Carl Lesnor Family Foundation.

Archipelago Books also gratefully acknowledges the generous support from
Lannan Foundation, the National Endowment for the Arts,
and the New York City Department of Cultural Affairs.

PRINTED IN CANADA

If the doors of perception were cleansed every thing would appear to man as it is: Infinite.

William Blake

The world is unstable, like a house on fire.

Linji

Difficult Light

One

That night I spent a lot of time awake. Beside me, Sara wasn't sleeping either. I looked at her brown shoulders, her back, still slender at fifty-nine, and found solace in her beauty. From time to time we held hands. In the apartment nobody was sleeping, nobody was talking. Occasionally someone coughed or got up to pee and then went back to bed. Our friends Debrah and James had come to keep us company and had settled down on a mattress in the living room. Venus, Jacobo's girlfriend, had gone to his room to lie down. My sons Jacobo and Pablo had left two days earlier in a rented van, heading for Chicago. From there, they'd flown to Portland. At one point I thought I heard the faint sound of Arturo, my youngest son, strumming his guitar in his room. In the street I could hear the nighttime shouts of the Lower East Side, the familiar tinkle of breaking bottles. At about three in the morning, two or three Hells Angels thundered by on their motorcycles from their clubhouse two blocks away. I slept almost four hours straight, dreamlessly, until I was awakened at seven by the knot of grief in my belly at the death of my son Jacobo, which we'd scheduled for seven that night, Portland time, ten o'clock in New York.

Two

I kissed Sara, got up, made coffee. Unaware I was even doing it, I started looking at the painting I was working on. It was too early to call the boys, who'd spent the night in a motel near the Portland airport. The subject of the painting was the foam churned up by the propeller of the ferry as it leaves the dock, when the motor begins to roar in the seething green water. The emerald color of the painted water was pale, superficial, I thought, like a piece of spearmint-flavored candy. I hadn't managed to render it so that, subtly, imperceptibly, you could feel the depth of the abyss, feel death. The foam looked beautiful, incomprehensible, chaotic, separate yet inseparable from the water. The foam was good.

I'd begun the painting a year earlier, in the summer of '98. I used to spend entire days on the ferry while I was working on it, traveling back and forth between Manhattan and Staten Island again and again, sometimes drinking beer, always gazing at the water. I even made friends with some of the buskers on the ferries, and with Louis Larrota (whom I teasingly called Luis Bancarrota in reference to his empty wallet, though

5

he spoke neither Spanish nor Italian and didn't get the joke), the only person who still made a living shining shoes on the ferry. Even now I can hear him calling "Shoeshine! Shoeshine!" along the passageways of the ship. The number of his customers was dwindling, as most people had started wearing sneakers. Once the sunset blazing behind the cranes of New Jersey and crisscrossed by seagulls had burned out, I'd make my way back to the apartment.

I married Sara when we were both twenty-six years old. We lived together for another fifty, until she died of heart trouble a little over two years ago. It's hard to explain, hard to understand, but the women I desired who were not her, both those I never had and the very few I did end up sleeping with – without Sara's finding out, of course, as that would have been the end – they were all her. Those affairs took place only during our first two years together, when our relationship, still plagued by substantial gaps and misunderstandings, was not yet solid. After that, I was utterly and effortlessly faithful.

She had affairs of her own, I think, but those, if she had them, occurred many years later. One afternoon, after we'd already moved to New York, I saw her in a café holding hands with a woman from work. I asked her about it that night, and she neither denied nor admitted it; she said only that relationships between women would always be a mystery to men. I didn't find that particularly reassuring, since there's holding hands and then there's *holding hands*, but as the years passed I gradually forgot about it. The second time was when she was in Jamaica with James and Debrah. For some reason, I couldn't or hadn't wanted to go on that trip, and James accidentally let slip an anecdote that implied that Sara had had a fling with a young man on the island. I asked her about that one too, but that time she told me I was crazy, how could I think such a thing. But even today something tells me that affair did happen. Sara wasn't exactly inhibited, especially after a few drinks. True or not, in any case, I was torn up about it for a long time, but I ended up getting over that too.

Jealousy, maybe.

In any case, only our advancing age could diminish the desire we always felt for each other. I've never been all that good at distinguishing between love and desire, so I can say that we had a lot of love all our lives. And I was always happy to see her again, even if we'd been apart only a few hours. When I came home, back from the ferry, she would also be back from the hospital where she worked, and we would chat a while as we lay in bed; I would tell her about what I'd seen in the ocean, and then we'd go check in on Jacobo and the boys.

Three

We arrived in New York in 1986. In 1983 we'd left Bogotá for Miami, where we'd managed to spend three long years, years I don't regret at all – they weren't bad ones. I'd first been to Miami and the Keys on a previous trip and wanted to paint them. You could say I went to Miami looking for water and light. We both enjoyed the sea enormously for those three years, though we hated the city's spiritual poverty at the time. And eventually we decided to take the three boys to New York.

In Miami I painted a series of oil landscapes, studies of light and water, fifteen canvases two meters square, which I used to put together a solo exhibition on Key West. Some were abstract seascapes as seen from the Overseas Highway; others depicted the turbulent seas of Miami: the lighthouse, Crandon Park, downtown. Soon after we arrived, Sara and the boys bought themselves a dilapidated little catamaran and sailed on the weekends, hugging the shore, almost touching sand, really, but enjoying it as much as if they were traversing the Atlantic.

I turned forty-three in Miami.

Later, our friends there – we made only a few friends, but they were good ones – told me that the city was changing a lot, becoming less provincial, that the rednecks had left and the influx of people from other countries had improved the atmosphere, that even the new generation of Cubans was a little less obtuse and suffocating. Maybe so. And yet neither Sara nor I would have gone back. The boys wouldn't have wanted to return either. Actually, after two years in New York they weren't really boys anymore: Jacobo was eighteen and was getting ready to study medicine at NYU; Pablo, sixteen, was in an alternative high school at 23rd and 8th, with kids who had rings in their noses and ears, and was poring over college recruitment materials; and Arturo was fourteen and had pushed to get into La Salle, at Second and Second, for the sole reason that it was half a block from the apartment we lived in after what happened, so he could have more time to sleep. Going to bed late, getting up early, playing guitar, and drawing constantly – that's what he liked back then. Anyway. It was good while it lasted, the Florida period, but it was also enough. I managed to work a lot – Miami's crude, unsophisticated atmosphere back then was even helpful, in a way: I was able to immerse myself deeply in the bubble that my work entails (or used to entail, rather, since over the past year and a half, now that I'm seventy-seven, my eyesight has gotten too bad, so I've stopped painting and started writing instead, with the aid of a magnifying glass).

Our first apartment in New York was a cramped place on West 101st, a block from Central Park. The park was the only thing good about the place, which was on the edge of a poor Latino neighborhood and was loud at night. Broken bottles, shouted insults in English and Spanish, a dense human fog that kept me awake, especially since I'd just arrived from Miami, a city that seemed to have been built entirely alongside golf courses. If sleep was elusive, painting was impossible. The first months in New York were tough, really tough, not for Sara and the boys but for me, with my need for light, space, silence, and other trivial things a person comes up with at that age to make life more complicated.

Back then, I didn't want to be in Miami or in Bogotá or in Medellín or there on 101st Street or anywhere else. I'd go out early to wander through the park for hours and remind myself that I had to pull myself together, start working again, put on a cheerful face for Sara and the boys, who were happy in New York, though they were worried about the funk I was in. Sara had found a job as a counselor in a hospital – she'd studied sociology in Colombia – and realized that the neighborhood we lived in was what was bringing me down, maybe its ghetto vibe, and definitely the lack of space in the apartment. In the living room, the leg of my easel practically touched Arturo's shoulder as he lay on the carpet with his blasted Nintendo; and when all three boys were home, they made so much noise that, in combination with the cacophony of the street, they drove me away from my easel and paints and out into the park to look at the trees.

I liked the trees in Central Park, though they made me nostalgic for the trees of my own country, for the jungles of Urabá, which I knew so well, since one of my brothers had had a farm in that area and ended up living out his last days there. These trees were beautiful, certainly – stately old elms or oaks, for example – but practically toy-sized compared with the kapoks and cashew trees of Urabá, and they made me a little sad. And when I wasn't in the park, I would go to Coney Island, an hour or so by subway, which I'd discovered early on and which I found amazing, as everyone does. (There's a photo of Freud – him amazed, too, I think – on the boardwalk.) Afterward, back in the apartment on Second Street, I started my series of seascapes of the New York harbor, including paintings of the ocean at Brighton Beach and at Coney Island.

Sara came home from work one day and said, "Want to take a look at an apartment that's for rent? It's downtown, near Houston. At Second Ave. and Second Street. It's big. Rundown. Expensive. The windows look out over this gorgeous cemetery. Marble Cemetery, it's called."

I asked if it had good light and she told me it did, and we went to see it with the boys. It didn't seem too expensive to me, considering its size, but it was dilapidated. Filthy, even. It needed a good cleaning, some paint, and an exterminator. Large windows, excellent light. A spacious living room where we'd have no trouble fitting the boys and their electronic devices, a sofa, two armchairs, and my studio.

And things worked out really well. We fumigated the cockroaches and some died, but most of them stayed on with us. When you turned on the light at night, there they always were: small, abundant, swift, scurrying for crannies to hide in. We kept things squeaky clean and I fumigated again from time to time, put out borax, crushed them with my shoe, but nothing worked: when you turned on the light, there they all were. In old apartments these insects are as hard to snuff out as life itself. To get rid of them entirely, you'd have to tear down the building and douse the rubble with gasoline . . . or napalm.

I like plants and have a bit of a green thumb, so I got some ferns and palms, and soon the place started to take on a jungly atmosphere. We bought a parrot in a pet shop on Bleecker Street for two hundred dollars, and the boys named her Sparky. She screeched like crazy, never allowed herself to be tamed, and had the run of the apartment. Years later we got Cristóbal, the cat, who scared her one day, and Sparky flew out one of the windows that looked over the cemetery. The parrot stayed there a week, living in the trees and screeching loudly. She never wanted to come back, however much we called to her from the windows. Until one day she was gone.

"She probably went to South America," I told the boys, hoping to cheer them up. "She'll be eating chontaduros on the banks of the Chocó."

"Chonta-who?" asked Arturo, who wasn't familiar with the fruits of that palm tree and never missed an opportunity to joke around, even in difficult moments.

In the apartment on Second Street, my spirits started to rise again. I walked along the urban and semiurban shores of Brooklyn and New Jersey and took photos and made paintings of them. I painted a motorcycle I found half-buried on a beach and covered with seaweed. I liked the way the things man abandons deteriorate and start to become inhuman and beautiful once more. I like that dividing line. A sort of mangrove swamp. I did an eight-canvas series on horseshoe crabs, which wash up on the beaches of Coney Island, die there, and lie on the sand, becoming empty shells and then, quickly, dust, beside the flip-flops and shards of plastic containers that will last for centuries before they too finally turn to dust. The subject of those paintings, though I never said it, was obvious and magnificent and in any case quite pretentious or ambitious or whatever you want to call it – they were about the shadowy abyss of Time. Horseshoe crabs aren't beautiful in the least, and they haven't evolved for millions of years, along with cockroaches and crocodiles. I once read on the Internet that they aren't even crabs. They look like crustaceans, but they're actually more closely related to spiders and scorpions. The oldest horseshoe crab fossils are from about 450 million years ago.

The paintings had only enough glimmers of light that you could just make out the shape of the poor crab's carcass. And though they did sell, it was with great difficulty and for very little. Many years later they began to change hands for astonishing amounts of money. I still have one – the best one, in my view – hanging in my studio. It grows gradually

13

more imprecise and abyssal as my eyesight declines and I, too, advance toward dust.

"Heading deeper and deeper into tenebrism, are you? Pretty soon the canvas will be solid black," said Sara, teasing me. "Don't listen to me," she added hastily. "Of course I like them."

I enjoyed nearly two years of artistic plenitude, a happiness that also brought with it pangs of anguish: I was finding treasures everywhere, like someone for whom the stones in the road were suddenly gemstones. How could I have known what was coming! Misfortune is always like the wind: natural, unforeseeable, effortless . . . I was painting better than ever, and at times I became so intensely involved in my work that I forgot to smoke and drink coffee. I painted the seaweed-draped motorcycle – also somewhat tenebrist, though now with some flecks of color. In New Jersey I found a rusted children's tricycle in an empty lot at the edge of the water, and I also painted that, very large, but this time awash in so much light that you could hardly see the tricycle. (Two years ago I saw the painting in a museum in Rome, where they'd invited me for some sort of ceremony, but I had to look at it out of the corner of my eye, as the disease had started by then and the center of my vision was blurry. I liked it, that tricycle, when I saw it again all those years later, but I would have liked to go over certain parts of it that could have been done much better.) I'd also started taking photos of the abandoned roller coaster at Coney Island – the one they later tore down – overgrown with

14

purple flowers. Morning glories, they're called in English. I planned to paint a series of large paintings with close-up views of the structure and the flowers from angles that would upend the hierarchies of size and perspective and toss off the yoke of obligatorily looking either outward or inward. I prepared the canvases for the roller coaster. I'd have to paint the flowers real pretty, of course, so the paintings wouldn't be too hard to sell. A person's got to make a living.

It's sad now to be writing the jokes that I was telling up until two years ago, when Sara was still alive. "Something vaguely resembling a joke," she would have corrected me. And then the taxi carrying my eldest son was hit by a pickup driven by an intoxicated junkie at the corner of Sixth Street and First Avenue, less than four blocks from the apartment, and I, and Sara, and all of us, were plunged into the deepest hell.

Four

I didn't stop painting. I never stopped painting, not until recently. I finished the paintings I'd started, and I even prepped more canvases and started new ones, but for a long time it was a reflexive act, like the way they say some people keep walking after their head's been cut off.

So many years have passed since then that even the pain in my heart has gradually dried up, like the moisture in a piece of fruit, and only rarely now am I suddenly shaken by the memory of what happened, as if it happened yesterday, and swallow hard to contain a sob. But it does still happen, and I nearly double over with grief. But at other times I think of my son, and then I feel such warmth that in those moments it even seems to me that life is eternal, restful and eternal, and pain is an illusion.

Whenever I got deep like that, Sara would look at me with some amusement. Even now I can hear her voice teasing me: "Let me make sure I've got it all straight, David. So pain is eternal and life is an illusion? No, wait. Life is . . . ?" That's why I almost never go back over these lines with my magnifying glass, because it's pointless to try to see where

I'm on target, if I am at all, and where I'm being a moron. It's best to just keep going. And I don't have much time to go back over things anyway: I'm old now, and for some time I've been rapidly losing my eyesight.

Also, truth does not exist and the world is music.

Today I live by myself in a house in the outskirts of La Mesa, a city of thirty thousand in central Colombia. Sara died here two years ago. The back patio looks out over a deep, wide valley with vultures or buzzards or whatever you want to call them soaring overhead. Sometimes the vultures swoop low in the air, only a few meters from the cliff behind the house, above the abyss, and if my vision were good enough I'd be able to see how they move their flight feathers, changing direction or altitude, how they enjoy the World. (I see them very clearly and yet I can no longer see them. Where, then, is the World? Where does it perch?) Some people find it unsettling that beyond our garden, just beyond the orange and tangerine trees that Sara kept so well pruned and fertilized, there yawns such depth and vastness that it seems as if it might swallow everything up, like a terrifying symphony.

I am relatively healthy. More bothersome than my failing eyesight is the poor circulation in my legs, especially my left one, which causes sharp tingling in my fingers in the wee hours of the night (I don't know why it prefers those hours). Apart from that, everything is in decent working order. I lost my teeth to gum disease ten years ago and got dentures. I bought the best one available, super pricey, the Porsche of dentures, Sara used to joke, adding reassuringly that they were a major improvement on the teeth I'd had before.

A woman of about forty-five, Ángela, comes every morning and stays all day, looking after the house and preparing food. Ángela likes to tell me that I'm not eating enough and that I'm skinny for my height, which I find amusing, as height-to-weight ratios should no longer be a concern once a man has hit seventy-eight. I've still got my memory, I'm lucid, and generally speaking people don't treat me like an old man. What has happened, though, is I've become detached from the affairs of the world of the featherless biped, and I consider few or none of them truly important. Up until the situation with Jacobo, I was deeply invested in what people thought of my work, reading the reviews with an eagerness that now seems absurd, convinced I wasn't gaining enough recognition in the art world. And it was true: for a long time, my work was not valued. And as it happened, my son's long torment coincided with an immense, sticky swell of recognition that I did not want and that seemed to have chosen that precise moment to arrive for the sole purpose of exacerbating our affliction, like a drag queen or a monkey or a lunatic at a funeral.

Along with that recognition, though, came the money we so desperately needed.

Jacobo's intense pain started three years after leaving the hospital. The doctors had warned us: the worst thing might be not that he would never walk again, but the physical discomfort he might begin

18

to experience at any moment. The pain gradually became chronic and increased in intensity, to the point that there were days – not all of them, thankfully – on which we had to tiptoe into his room and speak in whispers so he didn't moan and tremble at the noise.

My eldest son spent the first three years after the accident wanting to walk again and striving toward that goal. Then he lost hope, and after that, and as the pain became chronic and increasingly unbearable, he started wanting death to come for him. He'd rather it happen in his sleep, he told Sara once, but it would also be okay if it took him when he was awake.

Five

I couldn't have stopped painting even if I'd wanted to, as our medical expenses, even with health insurance, were significant. We adapted the apartment so that Jacobo could move around, and many of the pulleys and other equipment were expensive, and the insurance didn't cover everything. Then came the physical suffering, and the expenses went from significant to astronomical. When someone starts feeling such acute pain, the most important thing is to stop it, to alleviate it somehow, and even if you have only partial success or none at all, it's quite costly.

The acupuncturists, for example, who never did any good, were expensive – the more Asian they were, the more they cost – and insurance didn't cover them. I remember for about a year we paid an acupuncturist from Chinatown three hundred dollars for each weekly session. Fourteen thousand dollars to Dr. Shu ("Doctor Zapato," Jacobo started calling him near the end), who had an office on Mott, until Jacobo himself said it wasn't worth it and we should stop wasting money on the guy. By then the persistent agony had soured the poor boy's spirit. Oh, and that's not even counting the cost of Dr. Shoe's so-called medicines, little black pills about the size of Colombian beans, very bitter, that had to be chewed very slowly so they'd be effective in combination with the needles they poked into Jacobo's scalp and everywhere else, leaving him looking like a penitent or a porcupine.

In the beginning there was a lot of equipment: not only the devices intended to permit Jacobo some degree of physical independence in daily life, but also a sort of gym we installed in one of the bedrooms, where, despite the doctors' gloomy prognosis, the boy did his exercises till he dropped with exhaustion, hoping he would manage to walk again through sheer will. It was a hope we all shared at first. After watching him struggle and suffer like a broken monkey for hours on those bars and rings, we thought he was showing signs of increased mobility, and he himself said he was starting to feel his toes again. But it was all in vain.

It's a cruel cliché: the last thing you lose is hope.

Pablo used to work out with him and grew quite muscular. He was inspired not by vanity, of course, but so he wouldn't hurt his brother while carrying him from the shower to his bedroom or when settling him into his wheelchair. A while later Pablo started getting tattoos, and so we ended up with a gigantic boy with a sculpted body, his massive arms and shoulders adorned with gorgeous scarabs and orchids, and with a way of being that was as gentle as water and stable as rock. Jacobo got muscular too, from all the exercise, though just in his shoulders and arms, while his legs looked withered and sad. Arturo, who didn't exercise at all, except for a stint playing ping pong in high school, was always tall and lanky like me.

Our two eldest resembled Sara in personality and physical appearance more than they did me, though they had a bit of both of us. Neither of them experienced the recurring periods of melancholy I've endured since childhood, and the boys always knew to accept it without question, just as Sara did, even though they couldn't understand how a person could suddenly get so dark and silent for no reason. And the biggest paradox was that most of those blue periods, which were in large part imaginary, gradually disappeared after the disaster. That insistent suffering – his, mine, all of ours – ended up sweeping away the worst thickets of foggy cobwebs in my soul, the densest, most imaginary ones, and left me stripped of arbitrary sadnesses.

I looked at the ferry foam a while, walked into the exercise room, and thought about how we could give all that equipment to one of Jacobo's many friends. The pulleys, I mean, as Pablo would definitely want to keep the weights and springs and other apparatuses so he could stay in shape.

I returned to the studio to look at the painting again.

He always had a lot of friends, Jacobo did, and that didn't change after the accident. Quite the opposite: in addition to his old friendships, his young comrades in misfortune started coming to visit. They showed up every day, in all sizes, colors, and personalities, all of them in wheelchairs, most of them trying to endure as best they could the physical pain that plagued them constantly. Jacobo had met them in one of those support groups that Americans are so fond of and that Sara and I resisted so long until we realized they were actually useful.

I remember one young man of about eighteen, exceedingly polite, who was paralyzed from the waist down just like Jacobo, but in his case thanks to complications during a surgery. He always talked like a doctor.

"How are you, Mr. David? Pleased to meet you. I'm Michael O'Neal."

I shook his hand and asked how things were going.

"Just so-so, Mr. David," he told me. "I suffered from adhesive arachnoiditis, a silent complication that may present in six hyphen sixteen percent of patients who undergo this lumbar surgery or a follow-up procedure, who may then experience a second complication, paraplegia, as the most common symptom of arachnoiditis is persistent pain in the lower back. They operated on my spine to treat herniated discs that developed as a result of the adhesive arachnoiditis, diagnosed by means of magnetic resonance imaging, and which affected the cauda equina..."

"I'm so sorry, Michael," I said.

"Same here, Mr. David. . . . Cauda equina. Then, despite a mechanical cleaning and surgical debridement, I presented with irreversible paraplegia with diffuse spinal affection due to serous fluid remaining in the wound bed. The intersomatic implant inserted during my first surgery was removed, and treatment concluded with the reinstrumentation of posterior stabilization, with a persistent neurological deficit. In other words, Mr. David, I was paralyzed, and ironically the pain is incredibly intense, intense and very persistent, and I feel it in my legs, which don't actually have any feeling. If they stabbed me in the leg, I wouldn't feel a thing, Mr. David, but this pain keeps me awake at night." He finally trailed off and fell silent, staring out the window at the trees in the cemetery, overwhelmed by suffering.

After finishing high school and wandering around Latin America and Europe for a couple of years, doing a lot and not doing much of anything, I'd studied medicine at Antioquia University in Medellín and could make some sense of medical jargon. I dropped out not because the profession didn't appeal to me – in fact, I was quite drawn to it – but because of my passion for painting. I transferred to art school against everyone's advice, as I seemed to have no ability or talent for the arts. But those years in medical school were hardly a waste, despite what everyone said, not just because my knowledge of anatomy proved quite useful in my work but because in my view it is always – always and without exception – better to know than not to know.

"I'm very sorry, Michael," I repeated, and Jacobo, who experienced the same sort of pain, looked at me with his large brown eyes, very intelligent and bright – and all the brighter in contrast with the thick black beard he was growing – and winked at me, a wink of amusement at the way Michael talked, but mostly a wink of empathy and compassion.

The windows of the apartment, which was on the fourth floor, overlooked a historic cemetery – I can't remember if I said that already – with lush, leafy trees. When we moved in, the most recent grave was that of Ellen Louise Wallace, buried in 1975. Four years after we came back to Colombia, James would tell us that in 2006 they'd buried someone else, one Robert Chesebrough Kennedy, in one of the plots by the street. At the rear of the cemetery were two spectacular magnolias, the first trees to bloom in spring. The cemetery was enclosed by an intricate wrought-iron fence, and because the gate was always padlocked, no one ever went in and in winter the snow stayed pure and dazzling. Only the squirrels and birds left tracks in it. The rats, too, I guess, since back then the city was overrun with them. "AIDS has called in the bubonic plague as backup," I'd joke to Sara about the rats. "Really, though," I'd add, "a city without pigeons, squirrels, rats, beggars, or cockroaches couldn't have much going for it." "What a list!" she'd say.

Here in La Mesa, the sky just caved in. A massive hailstorm has started, and our house is old but has a tin roof in the rear, so it makes a tremendous racket. It's rare to get hail in La Mesa. This is the first time

25

it's happened in sixteen years. It's one of the most beautiful experiences there is. The destruction of the self, the dissolution of the individual. The air smells like water and dust and you are suddenly nobody.

It's so loud, you can't even write.

Six

Ever since they'd left we'd been in constant contact with the boys by cell phone. They'd made their first stop on the way to Chicago at a Holiday Inn in Clearfield, Pennsylvania, which they reached after five hours of driving. Jacobo couldn't bear the excruciating pain caused by the van motion any longer. It was for exactly that reason that we'd assumed in the beginning that they'd travel by plane, but he wanted to see a bit of the world beforehand, and not arrive at death so . . . abruptly. So they decided to travel to Chicago first, to see the countryside and then the Great Lakes, and take a plane to Portland from there.

Making the whole journey by car as they'd originally intended, forty-nine hours, with Jacobo in such pain, would have been impossible. They did New York to Chicago in two days, avoiding the freeways and taking secondary roads instead, where they could see the real countryside and not go from rest stop to rest stop, from the Seven-Eleven in one town to the Seven-Eleven in the next. The United States is an ugly place if you don't know how to travel it. When you go by freeway, if you're a passenger and fall asleep at the gas station in one town and wake up at the gas station in another three hundred miles away, it's as if you hadn't gone anywhere. It's exactly the same when you go from Holiday Inn to Holiday Inn, which the boys had to do, not wanting to risk an uncomfortable stay at an unknown hole-in-the-wall. It's like being trapped forever in the most tedious dimension of time that God ever created. Of course, like Sara, they've always enjoyed everything to the fullest, even backwaters.

"Hey, David, here in Clearfield they've got this place that holds the record for the world's biggest hamburgers," Jacobo informed me over the phone. Sometimes my sons call me David, and sometimes Dad, in English. "They've got newspaper and magazine articles about it framed on the wall. The burgers look like motorcycle tires topped with tomato and mayonnaise. We teamed up with two other guys to eat one, and we couldn't finish it."

They had a great time on those back roads. They blasted Led Zeppelin and AC/DC as they passed dairy farms or corn fields glowing in summer splendor. Venus had showed Pablo how to give massages, which were the only thing, in all the years of Jacobo's experience with cures and treatments, that had brought any real relief from the pain. When it became unbearable, they'd look for a place to park, Pablo would carry him to the back of the van where they had a cot set up, massage him for forty minutes or an hour, and let him sleep a while, and then they'd continue on their way.

Venus was a physical therapist, and that's how they'd met. She was from Santo Domingo, but she'd lived in New York since she was a little girl. She'd come every two weeks at first, and when we saw that Jacobo's pain lessened significantly for eight hours straight – which in turn allowed him to sleep well and get a little rest – she started coming every Friday. The therapy was inordinately expensive, eight hundred dollars for each two-hour session, of which insurance covered three hundred and fifty, but it was unquestionably worth it. Of course, as the years passed it became less effective, until eventually it was no longer a matter of seeking relief with the massages but instead of making the pain go from unbearable to less unbearable. And the relief faded more and more quickly.

"With that price, that name, and that figure," Jacobo would tease her back when they were not yet lovers, "your clients must ask you for other kinds of massages too."

If any other guy had said that to her, I thought, Venus, who did have a very beautiful body, might have been offended. But women never got mad at Jacobo.

She'd start the massages on his feet. I did a lot of charcoal sketches of the two of them, trying to capture the intimacy between people facing the horror of pain together. They must still be there in my notebooks, somewhere in the jumble of my studio. That was before they started closing the bedroom door, of course, when the romance hadn't yet begun and I could go in there to watch her work. Venus would start with the arches of his feet, as I said, then his ankles and calves, and stimulate the muscles until they twitched reflexively and relaxed. Jacobo couldn't have known what she was doing, as they'd inserted a titanium rod in his spine, locking the upper and lower parts together. He only realized that Venus had reached the area above the rod when she bent him forward a little and Jacobo could start to feel the area where he had some sensitivity.

Venus was a little darker than Sara and they resembled each other. People on the street would ask them if they were mother and daughter. Once, the Met had an exhibition of portraits found in the sarcophagi of the Roman colonies of ancient Egypt, and I thought I was looking at the two of them, their hair very healthy, black, and curly and their eyes very large, black, and slightly almond-shaped. I painted a retable of the two of them as mother and child, an imitation of those paintings, which had been painted on wood, and I gave it to Venus. At first she didn't want to accept it, and she almost cried with happiness.

Sometimes I almost forget she isn't my daughter.

Seven

"Did you call them?" Sara asked.

I hadn't heard her come in, and I jumped. I was embarrassed that she'd found me working so intently on the water in the ferry painting, as if nothing else were happening. But she too studied it a while. She had been crying, and her eyes were red and swollen. I felt compassion for all of us; my Adam's apple turned to iron and my heart weighed heavy in my chest. Our sorrow was like a dark cloud that endlessly expanded and now blanketed heaven and earth.

"You're not there yet," said Sara, referring to the painting.

"No, not yet," I told her. "It's only four-thirty in the morning in Portland."

They'd made their second stop on the way to Chicago in Sandusky, Ohio, on Lake Erie, the roller coaster capital of the world. The amusement park has seventeen roller coasters, Pablo told me, and apart from that, or because of that, it was a terrible place. As world capitals go, he said, I much prefer the town with the burgers. I think he, too, was beginning to feel the burden of what was about to happen, and he was having a hard time staying cheerful. Realizing that he didn't want to talk much, I passed the phone to Sara. I don't know what the boys were saying to her, because she hardly said a word, only "yes, yes, of course," and continued listening. "Pass me to Jacobo a minute," Sara said, and then she kept listening and saying "yes, of course, yes." And after a long time the phone went back to Pablo again and the conversation proceeded as before. Or maybe I do know, or can guess, anyway: they told her that the thing they were going to do was best for Jacobo, because he couldn't take it anymore; that it was a crime to remain in such agony and that we should think of it not as an ending but as the doors of his liberation, his redemption. That must be it.

Sara had a powerful spirit. When we arrived in New York, we spoke very little English, as we hadn't needed it in Miami. But within a couple of weeks she had finagled an interview with a medical company that had a contract with the city government to serve women who were at high risk of contracting HIV. Their offices were at Bellevue Hospital. Sara went through the interview – in English – with a doctor who later would become her friend and confess that she hadn't understood hardly anything that Sara had said. She'd hired her because of her friendliness, her easy smile, because many of her patients were Spanish speakers, and above all for having had the *cojones* (the doctor said it in Spanish, one of the two or three words she knew) to show up at that interview without knowing English. People with fortitude – that was definitely what was needed back then to combat what had become the most terrifying plague since the Middle Ages and that had people dropping like flies all around us. Sara was completely self-directed and steadfast. Her strength did not depend on the admiration or applause of others. It came from her very neurons, from her genes, from a childhood free of shadows – despite the hair-raising violence she'd witnessed in her hometown growing up – and from the unconditional love and affection she'd always had the good fortune to receive and always knew how to offer to those she cared about. And now this is starting to sound like an obituary . . .

Anyway. Here in La Mesa she took care of the trees and the gardens, garbed in gloves, tall rubber boots, and a straw hat, while I took care of the potted plants inside and in the courtyard. I filled the house with double-bloom azaleas, ferns, heliconias, bromeliads, and begonias, plus some climbing plants for a few walls that got enough light, along with the paintings and sculptures my friends have given me and a few works of my own that I've never wanted to sell, the furniture we'd brought from New York, and furniture and lamps I bought in antique shops in Bogotá. I've always enjoyed trying to find the equilibrium of objects, and it never ceases to amaze me the way they come to life if you understand the light in a space. In their relationship to light, so-called inanimate objects are as alive as plants, as alive as you or I.

I was about to dial Jacobo and Pablo in Portland when the house phone rang and Sara answered. A Belgian critic was preparing to write a book about my life and work and wanted to know if he could come by the following afternoon to talk to me and perhaps stay with us a couple of days. Sara hesitated only a moment; she told him I was in Colombia and would be back in a month. Without consulting me, she and the Belgian worked out an arrival date for him on the second Saturday of the following month at three in the afternoon, while I, who a few days earlier had called to cancel all my professional engagements and now wanted nothing to do with that sort of thing, gestured wildly at her that I didn't want to talk with anybody, no Belgian on any second Saturday of any following month.

"It'll offer a distraction and help us think about something else for a bit, which we'll need by that point," she said after she hung up, and I no longer had the energy to remind her that I'd never liked for other people to make decisions about my affairs. "Plus he sounded nice," Sara added.

Eight

I went to feed Cristóbal, who had been twining around my legs for a while. He was white with yellow eyes, he had two black spots on his back and one black ear, and he was big and plush, as if he were stuffed with cotton. He was a happy cat. We got him when he was a newborn kitten, he lived fourteen years, and he experienced pain only three times in his life: when the anesthesia wore off after he was neutered, once when I stepped on his paw, and when he suffered the pangs – sadly inevitable – of death. It's strange, though, because I feel like he's still around, even here in La Mesa.

The smell of the cat food – a wet paste of fish and flour – made me sick. I felt sorry for Cristóbal for having to eat it. I went back to the kitchen and we called Portland.

Conversation was difficult. I asked Jacobo what time it was there, he told me it was eight twenty, and we fell silent. How's the hotel? I asked, and he told me it was fine. Same as any other, you know? I asked him how he was and he told me he was fine, and again we fell silent. I asked

35

him about the pain, and he told me it was really intense at the moment but that Pablo was going to give him a massage. A long silence. I'm going to pass you to Pablo, he told me, and then pass me to Mom, okay? Love you, Dad, talk to you soon.

It wasn't any easier to talk to Pablo. I asked him when the doctor was coming and he told me seven at night – which I already knew but hadn't been able to think of anything else to ask. We had less and less to talk about. Silence began to coil implacably around us. I asked if they'd had any trouble when they turned in the van, and he said no. I'll pass you to your mother, I said, and their conversation was as fluid, and as mysterious to me, as it had been on other occasions. Though her voice remained steady, I saw Sara's eyes shining with impending tears. I decided to go out for a while.

Despite the large magnifying glass I use, I had to stop writing for more than an hour because I could no longer see the words clearly. And I write large, too, with letters about the size of a blackberry. When I can't see anymore, which happens more and more often now, I go lie down, ask Ángela, the woman who comes to help me around the house, to please put a damp compress on my eyes and forehead, and focus on listening to the sound of the birds or put on music. Of all the birds, I am fondest of the song of the ones we call *azulejos* – blue-and-gray tanagers. Though they have the same name in Spanish, the Colombian bird is not the same as the American blue jay: it is much smaller, though just as sprightly and aggressive. It has a shrill call, precise and somewhat elaborate, like piccolo music, and so high in pitch that it almost seems like some of the notes are inaudible to the human ear. It is complex, but not beautiful. And because it is so high-pitched, we don't pay much attention to it and instead notice birds with more earthly songs, especially sparrows, the most talkative species on earth: the chirping plague, you might say, the way pigeons are the flying plague. When I listen to music – which I do a lot – it's often guitar music: Albéniz, Rodrigo, Tárrega, Barrios, things like that, or also *The Magic Flute*, pieces by Grieg, or parts of the Ninth Symphony, which I still find dazzling after more than sixty years. In any case, in the future that looms before me I will be able to enjoy only the light of sounds, the light of memory, and light without forms, as my eyesight is in irremediable decline. I do have a future, I think: my family tends to live a long time, with many of my relatives having lived into their nineties.

I have no idea whether putting a cold compress on my eyes and forehead does any good, but you have to do something, I guess, and maybe it helps me rest. I've got what old people get: macular degeneration. Though it supposedly rarely leads to complete blindness, the rapid deterioration of my vision indicates that such will be my fate. A magnifying glass becomes necessary when a person loses sight at the center of the eye. The macula comprises about 5 percent of the retina and is responsible for some 35 percent of the visual field. The remaining 65 percent – that is, the peripheral area – is not affected by the disease. The magnifying glass helps compensate to a degree for the damage to the macula, as it allows you to rely more on the healthy retina surrounding the injured area to create visual images. When I get up, and before I sit down to work again, I go out onto the patio to look at the plants and trees.

The rear patio of my house is about six hundred meters square and – while we're on the subject – contains infinite visual images. The garden Sara created is spectacular. It is full of all kinds of palm, banana, and citrus trees, and all the varieties of heliconias, ferns, and orchids you could imagine. She became a real landscape artist, Sara did, here in La Mesa de Juan Díaz, and for more than ten years I was her only audience and the dazzled painter of her living paintings. Now Angela's husband takes care of the garden, and from what I can tell he does a good job, but it no longer evolves or changes; no longer do mossy stones appear, or ponds with lily pads and other plants already intact, or exotic plants that she obtained and that seemed to have flowered all of a sudden, in an instant, like fireworks . . .

When I think about all that and feel Sara's absence, feel the chill of the inescapable solitude of old age, I have to go lie down, shut off my soul for a few minutes as if blowing out a candle, and sleep.

Nine

I interrupted Sara a moment to tell her I was going out and would be back in a couple of hours, and to call me if she needed anything. She said that was fine, that I should go out, it would do me good, but not to take too long. I kissed her and she kept talking with the boys. Who weren't boys anymore.

I got off at Houston and took the train to Coney Island. I found the darkness of the tunnel horrifying; the train car was horrible; the people who got off and on were horrible. I stared at the floor so as not to look at anybody, until after an hour or so we'd arrived in Brighton Beach and I got off the train. I walked without looking at anything or anybody in Little Russia, and without looking at anybody I reached the boardwalk. When I lifted my eyes, there was the sea.

I've never been one to cry easily, and this moment was no exception. Two little sailboats, white like seagulls, were crossing the tranquil water, which was dark blue farther out and dark green where the waves rolled up and then unfurled their silks and brocades across the sand.

There were people on the beach, jogging, sunbathing. A young couple, probably about twenty years old, was throwing a ball for their black Lab, which hurtled into the water, swam like a seal to retrieve the ball, and then brought it back to them. Though I don't like paintings of animals, or rather of mammals, I imagined a painting in which the dog, plunging into the emerald-green water, would be only a stroke of black ink, like in Japanese calligraphy. There is no animal happier than a Lab at the beach. And I could no longer stifle my sobs, which erupted from me as if from the earth itself and forced me to sit down, still unable to stop the cold tears, hard as splinters, that were streaming down my face.

I took off my shoes, rolled up my pant legs, and walked for about ten minutes along the hard-packed sand, my feet in the water, until I reached one of the reefs below the Ferris wheel at Coney Island. I walked carefully along the sharp stones to where the water and crabs began. The crabs were rock-colored, and their movement made it seem as if the rocks were alive. I had been observing them for a long time, planning to do some oil paintings or maybe some etchings, studies of light and life commingling there among the brown and green rocks. I looked at my watch. It was after twelve thirty already. Time was barreling toward us as if it were about to dump a load of stones or bricks on us.

When I got back to the apartment, I found everyone visiting with Preet, who had come, as he did every Friday, to see Jacobo. Preet was the Sikh taxi driver from Jacobo's accident, and he'd come to visit him every single Friday since. He had a very long gray beard; an indigo turban, the same color as his shirt and pants; large, shining eyes; and an incredibly gentle gaze. When Preet came, we had to sit down and visit with him, offer him tea, and remain there, in near-silence, for exactly an hour. From time to time he'd ask, "And how are you doing, folks?" in that singsong Indian English that I so enjoyed hearing but found so difficult to understand, and we'd answer that we were fine, thank you, and you? and Preet would say fine, thank you, and then there'd follow a long, long pause that would stretch out until he'd ask once more, "And how are you doing, folks?"

Two days after the accident, he'd showed up at Jacobo's room in the hospital and said to us, "Hello, I am Preet."

"Sorry. Who?" Sara had asked.

"I was the taxi driver, ma'am. I am very sorry. Truly, truly sorry."

Strange things happen in car crashes. When Preet's taxi was hit by the drunk junkie's pickup, it was totaled in an instant. It was a miracle Jacobo survived, but even more surprisingly, Preet came out of it all utterly unscathed, not even a scratch. I bet he didn't even have his beautiful turban knocked askew, and that may very well be precisely why he felt so guilty, though it's hard to be sure since I found exchanging words with him as difficult as his smiles and friendly glances came easily.

"Preet means 'love' in Punjabi," he added.

"Oh," said Sara. "And it also sounds like 'pretty.'"

41

The taxi driver smiled, flattered. "Exactly, ma'am. Exactly."

We sat down and experienced the first of those long silences that we never got used to over the years. During the pauses, we'd watch him contemplating, perhaps somewhat anxiously, what he'd say next.

"Sikhs are monotheistic," he might say then, and not even Sara was able to come up with an appropriate response.

"How about that!" she'd say.

With Jacobo, Preet was significantly more outgoing. He'd grown quite fond of him – which wasn't difficult, given the boy's personality – and sometimes he patted his back and even said "son of a gun" and similar expressions, which for Preet were the height of comradery and informality. That was when he went into Jacobo's room to visit with him alone, of course. If Sara or I came in unexpectedly, the taxi driver would immediately return to his extreme politeness and geniality.

"Hello, Mr. David. Hello, Mrs. Sara," he would almost sing in his beautiful Punjabi accent.

When I came in after my trip to Coney Island, Debrah, James, Venus, Arturo, Sara, and Preet were in the living room. The taxi driver, of course, had no idea what was going to happen in Portland. Sara had told him that Jacobo and Pablo had gone away for a few days to visit some friends in Miami. Everyone but Preet looked a bit pale from lack of sleep. James, who was normally chatty, was silent, as was Debrah, who isn't the quiet type either. Debrah and James had been our best friends since we first got to New York. They didn't have children and had practically adopted ours as their own.

I shook Preet's hand and sat down to look at him along with everyone else. He looked like a god in that armchair: indigo turban, knee-length beard, and eyes so bright they were almost demented.

"Punjab is the land of the five rivers," he said after a while.

Sara gestured to me that we needed to talk. We excused ourselves and went to the kitchen, where she told me that the boys had just called to say that the doctor couldn't come to the hotel at seven p.m. and would try to make it at eleven. Everything had been pushed back at least four hours.

We fell silent. I embraced her.

"I don't even know whether that's good or bad anymore, David," she said and sobbed three times without making a sound. "Oh, God," she added, shaken, "and what if he doesn't come?"

Ten

Debrah and James came into the kitchen and the four of us hugged. I don't like collective displays of emotion, but this time it did me good, I think. Plus they're American and very different from us in many ways; they were our best friends, no question, and so we had to respect all that, even if it made me a little uncomfortable.

Debrah and James are still together. Besides ours, theirs is the longest-lasting marriage I know. They call to check in every two weeks, but since Sara's funeral two years ago they haven't been back to La Mesa: airports and airplanes are hard on the elderly. He's seventy-five, and she's seventy. The last time they called, they told me they were planning to go into a nursing home together, a notion I found appalling, of course, since to me that's basically deciding to breathe in the smell of your own and other people's urine day and night and day after day until you stop breathing altogether. But I didn't say anything.

Debrah and Sara worked together at Bellevue Hospital, which was how they'd met. James was a leftist lawyer, which in the United States means his clients were poor and he earned almost as little as them. James had put us in touch with a lawyer friend of his in Portland who specialized in these matters and would help us if anything went wrong, since Jacobo wasn't an Oregon resident and didn't have the right to that kind of assistance, and the doctor, Pablo, and Jacobo himself would actually be breaking the law and could get in serious trouble. It was the lawyer who had advised me and Sara not to travel to Oregon, to let the two boys go on their own, since having so many people there might draw attention to us. Sara flat-out refused, of course, and even got angry and cried, but she finally accepted it.

I misspoke. James actually earned less than his clients, since when they didn't have money, he gave it to them or lent it to them without expecting to ever get it back, and if Debrah didn't put her foot down he'd end up giving them her money too. Once I went down to the courthouse in Lower Manhattan to watch him work, and got to see him defend a Latina drug addict who over the course of the hearing gradually slumped more and more until in the end she was snoozing on his shoulder. She had robbed a neighbor for drug money and would have sold her children for a baggie of heroin. As he talked, the judge gestured to James not to let her fall asleep, and he had to push her upright and lift her head and her eyelids so she could look at the judge and the jury, which she did for a moment, lids drooping, before slowly leaning over again, her eyes now closed, and coming to rest on James's shoulder once more.

He is burly, tall, dark-complexioned, very intelligent, good as gold. Debrah is of Irish descent, from Ohio, with very blue eyes, petite and lively, as dynamic and swift as he is deliberate.

The drug addict and my friend touched me deeply. Deep, deepest respect, James. And now I don't even remember how it all turned out, if they put her in jail or what. The image that stayed with me was of the burly lawyer, formerly a football player at the University of Mississippi, and the emaciated junkie, who must once have been as beautiful as Venus, slumping, only half-conscious, at his side.

The four of us returned to the living room, where Preet was talking enthusiastically to Arturo about professional basketball. When he saw us, he straightened up, went silent, and smiled. Once again we all sat to look at him.

"Sikhism is the world's youngest religion," he said after a while. And this time it was Venus who remarked, "That's amazing."

Ángela just came in to ask me if everything is all right and if she and her husband can leave. "I left your dinner in the microwave," she said. "Don't even think about going to bed without eating, Don David."

She and her husband don't live here; they live in a little farm on the way to a village called Cachipay, and every afternoon they go to the main plaza to catch one of those little vans that weave up the gorgeous, verdant curves of the paved but potholed road to the village. I've gone to visit them a number of times on Sundays, and I go not in the car with my driver but in one of those vans. I like the atmosphere: everybody talks to everybody else as if they were all out for a drive and not riding public transportation. The only problem is that I have to hunch over a lot and my legs don't fit between the seats. I also like the farm: one and a half acres of coffee plants growing in the shade of pacay trees and a graceful species of acacia known as pisquín, and a wattle-and-daub house that is always neatly painted: white walls, red tin roof, and red window frames and doors. I drink coffee on the porch, gaze out at the trees, take a short nap in their bed, and return home. I don't think I'll take the van there very often in the future, as my declining eyesight makes me feel too unsteady to move around that way.

"Tomorrow I'll organize your papers," said Ángela.

As I fill these pages, I number them and put them in a Fab laundry detergent box I keep beside my desk. Because I have to write so large, I go through a lot of paper, and when the sheets don't fit in the box anymore, Ángela organizes them by page number and puts them in sheaves of one hundred on a large table I used to use for painting and engraving. The table looks beautiful piled with stacks of manuscript pages with blackberry-colored ink, the kind I like and which I prepare myself. There are thirty-odd piles now containing my memories of the years when Sara and I were young – the first five, I mean, which were such happy years and at times such conflictive ones, with that flood of hormones still rushing through our veins. And now the pages about Jacobo are starting to land there. I use special paper, thicker than normal, almost like etching paper, because I like to hear and feel the friction the paper makes against the fancy Montblanc fountain pen Sara gave me one Christmas.

But sometimes I wish I could paint again. Not those pathetic sketches I'd been drawing with my peripheral vision when I finally decided to quit and start writing instead, but big paintings, like the ones I used to do, paintings large enough to contain the whole world.

Eleven

We ordered sautéed chicken and noodle soup from a nearby restaurant. I hadn't had breakfast, but I still only ate a little soup and half a piece of chicken, which I chewed as if it were rubber. At the table, people were talking about Preet's visit, which had been difficult for everyone, and perhaps for that reason, and also because of our affection for him, we were having a little fun. Venus said that the orange turban looked better on him than the indigo one he almost always wore.

"Hello, I am Preet," Arturo said, almost singing. "We Sikhs do not recognize the caste system."

Yesterday afternoon they came here to the house to take my photo. I couldn't tell whether the magazine was about art, architecture, or interior design; the young man and woman, both of them quite attractive, wandered around the house taking photos of anything that moved or didn't. They captured me working at my table with my Montblanc and my magnifying glass. The magnifying glass is photogenic because it's big and square and black and is mounted on the table with a jointed arm that attaches to the tabletop with a clamp. They also posed me beside the climbing ficus that was gradually taking over one of the interior corridors. I think at this point I look like a statue by Alberto Giacometti, the sculptor: I seem to get skinnier every day, as Ángela says, and my figure has gradually turned to spirit or vapor. That is, drawing ever further from the things of this world and venturing into death, which does not exist, and into the infinite world we actually inhabit. If I could still paint, I would do a large self-portrait in which I would look like a mere shadow on a climbing vine that was solid, eternal, as if it were made of metal or stone.

There's another Giacometti: Diego, Alberto's brother, who designed some beautiful pieces of furniture in bronze. I once had a cousin make me a copy of one of Giacometti's tables, a slab of glass resting on a three-legged bronze tree with an owl perched on one of its branches. I had to travel to Medellín, where Ángel lived – he was a raging alcoholic but the best bronze worker around. It took him two long years, between occasional stints in the hospital for alcohol poisoning that almost killed him, but it turned out perfectly and it's in the living room next to a leather armchair we brought down from New York. When Ángel died three years later, I went to Medellín and was able to see him, emaciated, his beard neatly combed, wearing a tie, finally unburdened of the terrible suffering that alcoholics endure, in a sober coffin and surrounded by floral arrangements. I did a little altarpiece painting of his corpse, floating like Ophelia's on a river of flowers, almost primitivist, and because the flowers were painted in such a hyperrealistic style, nobody recognized it as my work.

The two young people stayed until dinner, ate, and left around nine. At one time I would have found that whole business with the photos and the articles and the endless questions about my work incredibly irritating. Especially during the years of Jacobo's suffering, it pissed me off to have to deal with that aspect of my work, which I found so unpleasant, and if it hadn't been for Sara, I would have closed the door and disconnected the doorbell and the telephone and let the chips fall as they might. But back then promotion was still a major part of my sales, and my sales were a major part of our lifestyle with Jacobo. Later, when my work was getting more attention and commanding higher prices, I began to agree to only those interviews that interested me and allowed me to say some of the things I wanted to say. Today, in my old age, it just makes me happy and makes me feel less alone to have young people in my home looking at my work, asking me questions, and taking an interest in Sara's garden and parts of my life.

At about three in the afternoon, Sara and I fell asleep for a few minutes, and when we woke up we made love lying on our sides, clutching each other so fiercely that we reached complete communion in pleasure and especially in affliction. I don't know how many times we must have made love in all those years together, Sara and I – thousands, I think, in thousands of ways and thousands of moods, both in happy times and in moments as awful as the one we were currently living through, and every time it was different, every time it was as if it were the very first. We fell asleep again for a little while, our arms still around each other and me still inside her. When we woke up maybe half an hour later, I heard the piercing song of some blue jays in the cemetery and, in the distance, down the street, a hoarse, ugly shout, like a death rattle: "Hey you, motherfucker!"

I once asked Jacobo about his sex life with Venus, and he told me that the first time he'd managed to ejaculate, the pain in his legs and cephalgia had been so intense that he'd nearly passed out. In time that physical pain began to decrease, he said, and eventually vanished entirely. Jacobo's injury was classified as T-10 complete, which means that he was paralyzed from the tenth thoracic vertebra down. I already knew a great deal about spinal cord injuries because of my years as a medical student, though I also did a lot of research online and in the libraries. I also got information from Michael O'Neal, Jacobo's young friend who enjoyed talking like a doctor.

"Not all patients with spinal injuries experience neuropathic pain, also known as, quote-unquote, phantom pain," Michael would say. "Indeed, the self-reported average for the prevalence of chronic pain in patients with spinal injuries is approximately 65 percent, of whom about a third report having severe pain, which, as in Jacobo's case and my own, is sometimes agonizing. And that's what you have to keep in mind, Mr. David: there's not much about these pains that's phantom-like. They're quite real, and sometimes the torment is unbearable, as if they were sawing at your waist or sticking your legs in a bonfire. Unbearable. Am I right, Jacobo?"

"Right you are, Professor O'Neal," Jacobo replied, and Michael smiled, flattered.

That day he showed up at around four, spoke very little, and stayed only a few minutes. It may be that Jacobo had told him about his intentions and Michael was expecting us to give him an update, as he asked whether Jacobo was home, but without conviction, and he didn't really listen when we told him some details about his supposed trip to Miami with Pablo.

Twelve

At four thirty they called again and said that the doctor wasn't going to come at eleven either, but at six in the morning the next day. They gave me the news, without details, and hung up quickly, as Jacobo was in a lot of pain and Pablo was going to give him a massage. They didn't talk to Sara.

"Tell Mom not to worry, he's a conscientious guy and will definitely be here at six," Pablo told me.

This time Sara didn't say anything, but only squeezed my hand hard and sat staring at a spot on the hardwood floor for a long while.

"What if he changes his mind?" she asked.

"The doctor?"

"Jacobo."

I didn't know what to say, didn't know what to think, didn't know what to feel. None of us wanted death – not him, not her, not me, not anybody – and life clings to this world with something akin to delirium.

The cockroach to its crevice, the plant to its chink between bricks or even to bare rock.

"With all this awful waiting . . ."

I went to the window. Down below, on one of the graves, was the statue of the Virgin Mary in a pose of profound peace. If only I were a believer, I thought, so I could go to a church right this moment, confess, no idea what for, pray . . . I'd love to have some tutelary gods, I thought, and sacrifice a rabbit to them, dedicate thick-smoked incense, leave them fruits, offer them flowers. But there was no Virgin for me, no tutelary gods. For me there were only those clouds, those pigeons that had just flown by, those trees, that jumbled void, that place whose borders cannot be identified, that blooming rose bush, that inexpressible abundance lulled by time and eternally harmonious, both when it was happy and when it was horrible.

"Everything's going to be okay. Everything's going to be okay," I told Sara.

"You think so?"

James and Debrah had gone to water the plants and change clothes at their apartment, which was uptown, at 125th and Broadway, and they'd be coming back to spend the night with us. Venus had gone out, beautiful in her white uniform, to see a patient on the Upper East Side. Arturo was working some nights as a sound technician in a well-known rock club in the Bowery called CBGB. He'd decided it was better to go in and clear his head a bit, so he was showering and getting ready. It was five in the afternoon.

Sara called her siblings. She had three sisters and two brothers. The men had all gone almost completely bald in their mid-thirties, while the women's hair seemed to grow more and more abundant, curly, shiny, and healthy. They were like the same woman painted by four different, though kindred, artists. Their complexions ranged from dark cinnamon – Sara – to a light wheat color – the eldest sister, who let her black hair fall in ringlets against her shoulders. I always liked my brothers- and sisters-in-law – the way they enjoyed life, their sense of humor, and especially their immense capacity for affection. *May your shell, like the snail's, be strong enough to make tenderness possible,* a poet once said, and that went for all of them. And, of course, I also liked the sisters for their beauty, and on many occasions I had to be careful not to look at them with desire or caress them, perhaps by accident, as if they were Sara. Two of them are still alive, both of them widows, both of them in Cali, and they are as pretty as ever. I call them from time to time and feel nostalgia, because it's as if I were hearing Sara's voice. The youngest brother is also still alive.

It was hard to talk to her siblings, who had no idea what was going on. Sara called them one by one, and every conversation went exactly the same. She'd try to make the usual jokes, but with effort, and I could tell the moment when, on the other end of the line, they'd ask her if everything was okay, tell her that she seemed strange. Sara would answer, her voice almost cracking, that everything was fine, that there were the inevitable problems of life, of course. Jacobo? Still in terrible pain, you know, she'd answer, but fine, everything's going to be okay, she'd tell them. Not to worry, she'd call them later and tell them about it, she'd add. And then she'd say: goodbye, goodbye, I have to rush off to work. Yes. I'll call you tomorrow. Yes. Yes. Yes. Bye, I'll call you, I'll call you, goodbye.

Thirteen

Everybody left. Sara went to lie down and I started looking at the water in the painting of the ferry. Fifteen minutes later, she got up, put on some yellow rubber gloves, grabbed a can of Ajax, and went to scrub the tub and tiles in the bathroom. (Debrah has always been amused by the way we pronounce it *ah-hahx* in Spanish, totally unrecognizable to an English speaker, and she often asked us to say it for her. She said it sounded like an ax falling.) I heard Sara energetically scrubbing the tiles, and then I heard her filling the tub. I heard her take off her clothing and I heard her slip into the water. My ear was always acutely attuned to all of Sara's movements. In other circumstances I would have gone into the bathroom to talk to her, to look at her. This time I knew that she wanted to be alone.

"What are you staring at?" she'd always ask in the bathroom when I got distracted and gazed at her too long: her breasts still high and firm at her age (which only happens with dark-skinned women, they say); her stomach flat with only two stretch marks on either side, which I even found beautiful; her lovely pubis, perfect, a nearly imperceptible shadow of fine hairs rising from it to her navel, where it created a climax of symmetry that took my breath away. I'd start from my trance and respond like one of the noble cat-callers of Cali:

"I'm not staring, I'm starry-eyed."

"You goof!"

Luckily it was summer and the days were long. In summer at a certain point you have the illusion that the days last forever. I didn't want night to come, because then I'd have to acknowledge that time was passing; that life was passing over us, crushing us with its wheels and gears. But only light, ever elusive, is eternal. And the light on the water beside the churning propeller of the boat, however much I studied it and reworked it, I was unable to find a way to capture it completely – that light that contains shadows, that contains death, and is also contained within them.

The landline rang and I didn't want to answer. The boys only called my cell phone, and I didn't want to face anything to do with my profession right now. I preferred to wait for Sara to come out of the bathroom and take care of it. The telephone kept ringing, and just when she, exasperated, yelled at me from the bathroom to please answer it, the phone wasn't going to bite, it stopped ringing. And when she came out in her robe with her curly hair damp, smelling of soap, it rang again.

It was her eldest sister, who'd been unsettled by the earlier call. She seemed surprised that Sara answered, since she'd thought she'd be at work, and Sara told her she wasn't feeling well and had decided not to go in. The flu, maybe. Yes, yes, yes. Of course Jacobo is fine, didn't I tell you he was doing fine? No, no, David went out just a moment ago, she said, and gestured at me to keep quiet, because she knew I was a terrible liar and didn't want to run the risk of passing me the phone. Headache, yes, she said, and a bit of nausea. I'm staying in bed. Okay, bye. I'll call you. What? Everything's fine, yes, haven't I been saying everything's fine? Okay, okay, tell everybody I said hi. What? Bye. Bye.

Implacably, night fell. The cemetery was sunk in half-light below us, and the sky turned dark blue.

Here in La Mesa, at that time of day, bats flit around the trees. The bats in this region are a small species with an innocent way of flying that reminds me of butterflies. They feed on bananas and tangerines. I go out on the back porch to watch them – or to know that they're there, rather, since I can't see much of them at this point – sitting in a director's chair with a beer that Ángela brings me before she leaves, served in a beer glass she keeps in the freezer. Behind the trees is the sheer drop that the vultures soar above during the day. This has always been the hardest time of day for me, ever since I can remember. It was in New York, too, where I'd go out to have a drink in silence in an empty bar. Here I sense the beauty of this hour, of course, its half-tints, and I love the presence of the bats in the gloaming, but sometimes I am engulfed with melancholy.

"You've gone autistic," Sara would say when she saw me light my first Pielroja cigarette, pour myself the rum or beer I drink every day, and sit lost in thought for a long while here on the porch. And though I don't consider myself particularly romantic or sentimental, it is true that it is at this time of day that I miss her most and am tormented by her absence.

"Hang on, hang on. What do you mean you're not romantic, David?" she might have teased me. "Sometimes you don't even let me breathe!"

The cemetery descended into total darkness, and in the sky the blue turned almost black.

Fourteen

I walked to a bar at one corner of Tompkins Square Park, at Seventh Street and Avenue B, where they filmed a famous movie scene in which a fat guy gets strangled with a cable.

There weren't too many people, and luckily the TV was off. I ordered a tequila and a beer. I sat down at a table in front of the bar where they strangled the fat guy, who thrashed around a lot, and next to the window, through which I could see the elms in the park, illuminated by the lamp posts, and a few people walking their dogs.

I've always been struck by New York dogs, which are so neutered and well-mannered that they seem like walking dead. They don't tug at their leashes, and it's unusual for one to start barking at squirrels, or even look at them – much less kill them – or chase after pigeons. Sometimes the owners walk in front and they're the ones who have to tug on the dog. I'd like someone to ask me about this subject in an interview so I could finally air my views on the difference between the *Canis zombis familiaris* of New York and the *Canis lupus familiaris* of Colombia or Latin America in general. But they never do. Instead, they drive me crazy with tedious, hard-to-answer questions about post-this and post-that or neo-this and neo-the other thing.

I stopped watching the dogs and downed my tequila. With a start, I remembered what was going to happen to us, what was happening to us, and it was like splitting apart inside, like suddenly recalling that I had been splitting apart inside for a long, long time. I drank the beer. Life was a horrible dream. As I write this, I'm thinking about the Sagrada Familia cathedral in Barcelona and how beautiful its architect's nightmare seemed to me; I'm thinking about *The Garden of Earthly Delights*. But none of that occurred to me then, in that bar. My horror was not aesthetic, or beautiful, or harmonious. In that moment, in that bar where they'd strangled the fat guy, the only thing I felt was an awful spike in my throat and a heavy weight behind my eyes, contained as if by a stone or concrete wall.

The Horseshoe Bar, it was – or is – called, like my dark, and now famous, tenebrist crabs.

I went back to the apartment and we called the boys. Pablo told me that Jacobo had been uneasy since the doctor had postponed and was in intense pain. He had fallen asleep after a long massage and four pills strong enough to knock out a bull. Pablo was speaking to us from the reception desk at the Holiday Inn so as not to risk Jacobo's waking up and hearing him. When I asked him if he thought his brother was having second thoughts, he told me he didn't know. That it was possible, of course, because Jacobo had been very quiet after the last conversation with the doctor, and now he opened his mouth only to complain about the pain.

"I can't take it, Dad," Pablo said. "But, well, it's totally understandable, right? And whatever he decides, we're going to respect it," he added.

At around nine Arturo arrived with Ámbar, his girlfriend at the time. Arturo and I are similar in many ways, except that one: it's not that he's a womanizer, because when he's with a woman he's faithful to her, but that he's been with several. Not too many, really, no more than three, counting Ámbar, until he met the one he's with now, Stella, almost eight years ago – but more women than me, in any event. Ámbar's name was Maria, or something like that, and she'd changed it to something less bland. And she was gorgeous. More petite than Debrah, which was saying a lot, very lively and intelligent. She had nine little silver earrings in the perfect oval of each ear, one for each year of her age. She was always in blue-black lipstick, nails painted blue-black, blue eyelids, silver rings on every finger, fake snakeskin boots, white silk blouses, and leather jackets and vests and pants in winter; in summer, she'd wear silver chains around her ankles, black tank tops, black harem pants, and brightly colored sandals. All high-end stuff, as she was from a wealthy family. She lived with her parents in the West Village. A few months earlier, as soon as she'd turned eighteen and was old enough to do it, she'd gotten tattoos done on her shoulders, arms, and upper back: fifteen dark-red roses, the kind with tiny flowers that we call cecilias, about two centimeters in diameter, with a few leaves and thorns. Once, when she was there, I goofed and told Arturo in Spanish that Ámbar looked like a little piece of art to be put on a shelf, and the moron went and translated what I'd said for her!

She didn't get mad – I'd say she was amused or even flattered. I drew a lot of charcoal sketches of Ámbar and also did a series of etchings that I was really happy with. Especially because I greatly enjoyed doing them and could reflect all the admiration I felt for her audacity and creativity.

I've always preferred to do my more figurative works as engravings or in charcoal. For years I copied Rembrandt's engravings, which I've always found incredible. They turned out well, and Sara, to stroke my ego, would tell me they were going to throw me in jail for forgery. I still have a few of them, including the one of the sacrificing of Isaac, but I've torn the vast majority of them up. And I prefer oils for my large-format paintings, which at times are almost abstract, like the one of the ferry, or completely abstract, like the studies of light and water that I did in Key West, or in the New York harbor, and then in the peaks and chasms of La Mesa and its environs, and that are the bulk and perhaps the most significant part of my work.

(Substantial, I mean, not significant.)

"Hello, dear," said Sara. "And you, Arturo, weren't you going to work?" she asked, and he said he hadn't been able concentrate and had decided to come home to be with us instead. A friend had filled in for him.

Arturo and Ámbar went into his room and closed the door, like they always did, but this time I didn't hear the usual jokes or laughter, since they were always teasing each other and tickling each other like children, rather than anything serious or erotic, I always thought. That night Arturo played his guitar and she probably surfed or chatted on the Internet, or maybe slept, since I didn't hear her.

Fifteen

I started brushing Cristóbal. His favorite thing in the world, besides sleeping and eating, was being brushed. The fur that was left in the brush was so soft, clean, and white that I always told Sara we should save it and use it to fill cushions. This time I didn't make the familiar joke. There were jokes and stories that I repeated too often, and it was a miracle she hadn't left me, claiming spousal abuse. Sometimes I used the repetitions to entertain her:

"Did I ever tell you how happy I always was a child when my family went to the Gulf of Morrosquillo?"

"Only five hundred thousand times."

"Okay. So my dad had bought a fisherman's hut in Tolú, right on the beach, and every vacation the whole family . . ."

Sara would cover her ears and sing "lalalala" to drown me out. If one of the boys was around, she'd say almost severely, "You kids are crazy."

I would be quiet and wait patiently for her to stop singing and uncover her ears.

". . . and I've never been so happy anywhere else as I was there. I was about seven when we started going. When I woke up the first morning, I could hear the sound of the sea on the sand and I felt so happy that . . ."

Sara would shout, "Ay, no, no" and start lalalala-ing again.

She went to the kitchen to heat up the pieces of chicken left over from lunch and toast bread for sandwiches. She knocked on the kids' door and asked them if they wanted to eat.

"No thanks, Mom. We went to McDonald's on our way here," Arturo responded. In other circumstances he would have added, "That fucking garbage!" to mock me, as I'd turned my personal boycott of McDonald's into a matter of principle.

An insidious, subterranean silence had fallen over the house, a silence that didn't lift even when we spoke or made noise. Two years later I would hear that same silence, but on a massive scale, when the Twin Towers fell. From the balcony, Sara, the boys, and I watched them crumble and disappear. After they turned to dust and smoke and the smell of char, that silence pervaded the squeal of the subway cars when they took a curve, the voices of people in restaurants, the heavy traffic on Canal Street, the cacophony of trains and cars on the bridges, and even the sirens; that silence took hold of everything, and you would have thought that the noise of New York, as fundamental as that of the mountains of Urabá, had been conquered from within and vanquished forever. That wasn't the case, of course. It never has been.

I never thought I'd end up singing the praises of noise.

"You have to eat, even if you don't feel like it," Sara told me when she brought me sandwiches and salad. "Your cheekbones are starting to stick out."

I ate the sandwich and salad listlessly; I drank the puffed wheat shake that Sara had learned to make from some Cubans in Miami. Ten o'clock. James and Debrah arrived. Michael O'Neal called, "just to say hi." He didn't even ask about Jacobo. "Everything okay over there, Mr. David?" he asked, and I told him that everything was okay, thank you, Michael. He said goodbye and hung up.

Today I read back over these pages with my magnifying glass, at the risk of ruining the little eyesight I have left. I was struck by how sentimental I've grown in my old age. When I talk about Sara and me, for example, I tend unwittingly to select the best moments, to smooth over times that were sometimes quite rough. Our years in Bogotá, in particular, were complicated, thanks to the merciless self-absorption of young people who want to make what they grandiloquently call "works of art." Sara had to take care of the house, with three children, for almost three years, while I shut myself in to do battle with canvases that I sold once a millennium or so and for very little. Then they began to sell more often and for higher prices, but even if they hadn't – that is, if I hadn't sold anything at all – I would have stayed wrapped up in my own world and let other people starve or find jobs or whatever else.

The night that had fallen was going to be even longer than the one before. Sara had been talking to Pablo and Jacobo a long time, more than an hour. She hung up and then called them back a few minutes later. Sometimes I'd go to the phone for a bit, and soon say goodbye. She spoke to them in a quiet voice, not to keep me from hearing, of course, but because that's the tone mothers use to comfort their children. Sometimes it almost seemed like she was singing to them to soothe them or like her voice had taken on the cadence of a lullaby. "Don't pay any attention to ghosts, boys, there's no such thing. Don't be frightened by figments of the imagination. Death doesn't exist, boys. Jacobo will always be here with us. Don't be afraid, don't let yourselves be confused or frightened" – she must have said something like that, I imagine, because what else could a mother say? While I, who have always thought that life is all there is and that to lose it, as a poet says, is to lose everything, shut myself in the darkness of the bedroom so as not to hear or see anything for a few minutes.

I've always felt guilty about my inability to console others, especially when those others have been my children.

Time is strange stuff. Only a few hours stretched before us – less than eleven now – which would be full of more sorrow than everything that had happened to my horseshoe crabs in their millions of years of existence. And at the same time they were dead, empty hours.

Sixteen

I went to Bogotá for an eye exam. Sara and I had bought an automatic station wagon with dual-clutch transmission and comfortable seats, totally luxurious. She was the one who drove it, and she'd wanted a big car since she often had to transport bags of manure and other things for the garden. I also saw her load stones and bricks into that glorious car.

The only place I drove was in Miami, since there was no other way to get around that city: it has almost no public transport, and I was always going to the Keys to paint and take photos. A terrible driver. I learned at the age of forty-five, so I drove as if I were ninety: slow and gripping the wheel with both hands, just in case. In New York I traveled by train with all my gear, or, if I had to, I took a taxi.

After the accident, Pablo bought a pickup truck to help drive Jacobo around. In a way, he started living for his brother. I don't mean that he stopped having a life of his own, but he took Jacobo into account in every decision he made. For example, he turned down the scholarship offered to him by a university in Massachusetts, rejecting out of hand

71

any possible separation, and instead studied film and photography at an excellent, but less prestigious, university in New York. Because he's so talented, the genius of the family, it ultimately led to the same place, and he's had a fair bit of success in his work.

When Sara passed away, I hired Ángela's eldest son as a driver, and when I have to go to Bogotá or want to take a trip to Girardot – a somewhat dilapidated but charming city that swelters on the banks of the Magdalena River about two hours from La Mesa – I go with him and Ángela. We always stay in a five-star hotel there; Ángela and her son each have their own room and I have another. I'm very fond of the two of them, and I love seeing their admiring and slightly awed response to such luxury. Money has to be good for something, since in most of its other manifestations, like fame, it is unpleasant, aesthetically hideous or even revolting.

Like most doctors, my doctor in Bogotá didn't tell me anything new. He didn't know why my blindness was progressing so rapidly, since my macular degeneration wasn't the worst type. And when I asked how long I would at least be able to write, he told me he didn't know, that when I couldn't write anymore it would be because I couldn't write anymore, and that I should always make sure I had plenty of light when I wrote. As if I were doing it in the dark! In short, as I said earlier: I don't know anything, you don't know anything, nobody knows anything. The world is only cadence and form.

After the exam, which was both thorough and thoroughly useless, we had lunch in a restaurant in the historic area of town and took a drive through other sections of downtown. Bogotá is intense, and not particularly beautiful. It's vibrant, yes, but it's hard on its inhabitants, like a poorly oiled machine. I can't see the mountains that rise above it anymore, but once upon a time I used to explore and admire the detail of their shapes, their stones and trees, their massive verticality so close by, their vegetation that so often turns a marvelous dark blue, almost metallic, and its ever-changing skies. As is happening to me with so many things these days, all of that now quivers, turns to liquid, eludes me . . .

I have three people on call who work for me: Ángela, the housekeeper, who is not my woman but is Woman incarnate (without Whom nothing has ever functioned); her son, a voluble and loquacious driver of twenty-five who studied agricultural administration at a technical college and was never able to find a job in his field; and Ángela's husband, a gardener, quiet and courteous, who also takes care of all my household repairs, since his hands work miracles. I pay them well and they're good people, so I can count on them to keep me company and help me when blindness blurs all forms and I am left with only light, and to call my sons to let them know, and then everybody will take me to the La Mesa de Juan Díaz cemetery and bury me next to Sara beside one of those palm trees (most of which are already dead and whose tall trunks, thanks to municipal indifference, rise stark and bare of plumes, like the columns of ancient ruins) when the eternal light shines for me.

"This from the guy who always pretended to be so aloof," I can hear Sara comment. "And now we've got his-and-hers gravesites?"

Seventeen

Why bother going to bed if you won't be able to sleep? And yet at about eleven I went – what else could I do? From the bed I could see Sara at the bathroom mirror, rubbing almond-scented lotion on her legs, and once more I admired the beauty of her dark skin, the loveliness of her back. Her body hadn't changed much with age. The telephone, which she'd carried into the bathroom, rang, and she put on her robe, answered it, and spoke for a long time in a very low voice with the boys. She had a deep voice, the same color as her skin, and it could take on many shades of tenderness. I shut my eyes and thought about the pain that was living inside me at that moment and surrounding me like the flames in paintings of purgatory. I kept them shut a long time, observing the intense grief that engulfed me, and what I saw in my head was a fifty-nine-year-old man, intelligent-looking and polite, though somewhat distant – me, walking slowly at night, as if nothing were going on, engulfed in flames, down an empty street on the Lower East Side; and that same man, also engulfed in flames, in East River Park at six on a summer evening, perhaps smoking, leaning on the railing to look down at the river, amid pigeons pecking at the ground around him and seagulls and clouds floating in the air.

Affliction is not motionless; it is fluid and unstable, and its flames, which are not orange and red but blue, and sometimes a horrible pale green, torment you sometimes on one side of the body and sometimes the other, sometimes forcefully gripping your whole body until you find yourself silently screaming like that Munch painting where a person is wailing on a bridge. Physical pain is no more stable, according to the descriptions I've read and heard from Jacobo and poor Michael O'Neal. The metaphors they use are intense. "It's as if they were taking a saw and slowly sawing at my pelvis, Mr. David," Michael would say. "And sometimes it's like my legs are frozen and at the same time covered in burning coals. Honestly, I don't know if it's really worth being alive if it's going to hurt this bad. What do you think?" And our poor Jacobo talked about how sometimes it was as if somebody were crushing his toes in a vise. Or punching him endlessly in the stomach. In their descriptions, the two of them almost inevitably reached the very limits of language itself and arrived at the sort of pain for which "indescribable" is the last word uttered before all words have been exhausted and there remains only the mute brutality of reality.

And yet I have known – all of us have known – joy, even happiness. The harmony of the world is not smudged or sullied even in moments of the most awful horror. Goya knew that, and Bosch. When Sara died I wanted to die too, of course, and contemplated suicide. During the weeks that followed I often imagined going to one of the beautiful misty cliffs in this area and tossing myself off it. Two bounces on two boulders, and someone my age would have shattered to bits. Like the romantic old fool I am, I would have put on my good suit, the one I wear for awards ceremonies, and I would have waited, neatly dressed, and dead, and dirty, and sprawling, for the vultures to begin to trace their graceful halo above me.

Fifty years of sensual delight and spiritual joy – here I am forced by language, which is inherently clunky, to describe as two separate things something that in its simplest, purest form is only one – with a woman who could as easily live in tenderness and pleasure as she could create gardens of heliconias and ferns and palms and little groves of flowering sietecueros trees, and pools and lily pads.

There was a reason I wanted to jump.

Eighteen

When Sara came to bed, it was ten past eleven. I had spent a long time, my eyes firmly shut, studying the flames that inhabited me and seemed, or perhaps were, eternal. Time is elastic stuff governed by joy or suffering. Sara lay down naked, her back turned but pressed against me, and lowered her hand to caress me. I did not penetrate her: Sara opened herself and put me inside her and pulled my buttocks with her hands to drive me deeper into her and thus console me, console herself, and take comfort in our love amid the pain.

We slid toward sleep.

I dreamed it was one in the morning and the boys had called. Jacobo had eight hours left, if he didn't get scared and change his mind. Jacobo wasn't the sort to get scared or second-guess himself, but life has a power that resembles madness. Two thousand feet below the earth's surface, I've read, there are living bacteria. I answered the telephone and talked to Jacobo, who seemed to be making an effort not to cry, or maybe he was crying. He didn't ask me to pass him to Sara. He seemed to want to say something just to me and didn't know how to go about it. I suddenly saw myself engulfed in flames again. This time the image was of the fifty-nine-year-old man at noon, running – on fire and in silence – along the East River. A garbage barge moved past, the trash held down by a net. It was surrounded by wheeling seagulls, and it left a sour odor trailing behind it. I woke up and it was only ten to midnight and the boys hadn't called.

James and Debrah were lying on the mattress in the living room. Venus was in Jacobo's room. Ámbar had stayed with Arturo, and I thought I could hear the guitar and the sound of the computer keyboard. No Hells Angels motorcycles rumbled past that night. Sara was lying on her back with her eyes closed and her hands folded on her chest. I prized them apart to slip mine between hers, and the three hands slid down to rest on her belly, which rose and fell with her breathing under the fabric. At some point she had put on her pajamas. She wasn't sleeping. I always sleep naked, even now that I'm an old man, despite the cold, because pajamas always get twisted around me and keep me awake. Sara squeezed my hand without opening her eyes. I sat up a little to look at the clock on her nightstand: midnight. Now it really was midnight.

Here in La Mesa it's cold at times. My kids brought me an electric blanket that has become one of my most cherished possessions. At first I was bothered by the umbilical cord that connected me to the wall plug every night. That was after Sara died, of course, and the world went cold. They say it's slowing circulation that makes the elderly feel cold. But I got over that after a while and mused ironically that old people become children again, and that the electric blanket was the first sign of childhood circling back, the return to the most fertile womb, the womb that has no name. And now it occurs to me that if by some miracle I could ever paint again, the first thing I'd do would be to seek the absolute resonance of the circle of Zen calligraphy, but via the subject of the water and light and stones I once saw in the Apulo River, near Ángela's house. Words are so clumsy, as I think I said already. I have a crystal-clear idea in my head, even took some notes for the painting, thinking I would still be able to do it. Except that I needed my eyes to capture it, and I can barely produce these purple scribbles with the fountain pen Sara gave me.

The last time I tried to prepare a bottle of ink, I screwed it all up and had to ask Ángela to help me. I told her the proportions of the colors and it came out beautifully.

The boys also brought me a Basque beret that I've been wearing more and more because of the cold. Ángela tells me it makes me look dapper. Sometimes I sense in her that affectionate condescension that people often show to the elderly, though I could be imagining things, defensive. Anyway. What are you going to do? There are two famous paintings – I can't remember the painter's name right now, I think he's French – that are called *Portrait of an Old Man*, *Portrait of an Old Woman*, and what struck me, apart from the high quality of the painting, is that in old age we lose our names. It's not *Portrait of Monsieur Armand*, *Portrait of Madame Armand*, or whatever. "Old man" and "old woman" are enough, at a certain point, to explain everything about a human being. Geezer, codger, coot, graybeard, old duffer. Here in Colombia, "prostate." Insulting terms abound. The human ape is a mocking and merciless one. A great aunt of mine, Pepa, the cruelest ape I ever knew, had two nieces who were born blind, her sister Concha's daughters, and she called them "Concha's squinties."

The English nickname "old fart" is my favorite, though "coot" isn't so bad, either. And "squinty" is how I'm going to end up pretty soon.

Nineteen

At five past midnight, Sara got up to call Jacobo and Pablo, and Cristóbal came to bed. The cat almost always slept in Arturo's room because he loved the epic chaos in there, which offered him an assortment of odd places to curl up in. But when Ámbar was there, he was afraid of the kids' roughhousing, or just didn't like their bouncing and shaking, which didn't agree with his temperament, and he'd come sleep with us instead. He came up onto the bed, rumbling like a tractor, and curled up on my legs, as heavy as a bale of cotton.

When Cristóbal died, Sara framed a photo of him sitting in all his white elegance beside a vase of freesias, and she kept it on her desk. It's still here, in our house in La Mesa now, Cristóbal beside his freesias, on one of the bookshelves in the library. When we first got here we had a black cat called Espartaco, the most brilliant black I've ever seen on an animal, but he didn't last long. We had him neutered, of course, but here the cats wander around on the rooftops and through the streets, and they often vanish without a trace, like he did, because they eat poisoned rats or get hit by cars or are killed by dogs or people. "It's like the Wild West for cats," Arturo once remarked.

I've never been much interested in painting animals, except for things like crabs, seashells, and snails, which are almost minerals – and almost flowers, too, or at least snails are.

I carefully shifted the cat a bit so he wasn't crushing me quite as much. Twelve past midnight. I couldn't stop looking at the clock. Time was screeching and tearing into us with its gears and barbs. Sara was talking on the phone in the bathroom in her velvety lullaby voice. Twelve fourteen. Out on the street someone shattered a bottle against a wall or against the ground. When we first got to the apartment, there had been a lot more noise on the street, more bottles broken against walls and pavement, more insults and shouting, but the neighborhood was gradually changing, becoming trendy, and there were art galleries and fancy restaurants. People called it the East Village now, not the Lower East Side. The streets smelled less like urine, and there were fewer people sleeping on the sidewalks. You rarely saw human excrement. "It's both good and bad," said Pablo, who feared the neighborhood would all get pretentious and expensive and kind of fake, like the West Village or Soho, which was in fact what eventually happened.

Cristóbal left the apartment only twice in all his fourteen years: once when we took him to be neutered as a kitten, and again when I, wanting him to experience the Big Wide World, took him up on the building's roof one morning. The poor animal was so panicked at seeing the blue sky above him, the dizzying scale of the universe, that he flattened himself against the floor until he looked like a swatch of fur, as if the sky itself were crushing him. I quickly carried him back down to the apartment, and he hid as far back as he could in Arturo's messy closet and stayed there for two hours in the dark, his pupils dilated.

Sara came out of the bathroom.

Twelve eighteen. The second hand was over the six.

"What happened?" I took a moment to ask, and she also took a moment to answer.

"I'm not really sure," she said at last. "I think they're scared."

"Oh. Yes," I said, and the flames – blue, yellow, red, horrible green – leaped up within me, torturing what felt like the walls of my soul, and seemed to lap at my spinal cord and brainstem and cerebellum and cortex. We turned off the lamps on our nightstands and went to bed hand in hand. I was uncomfortable because of the cat, who was crushing my legs again, but that discomfort also seemed to offer some consolation and companionship. I pressed my face into Sara's hair and breathed in the clean scent of her, her warm coolness, if you can put it that way, as if I hoped she could calm the blaze.

I must have fallen asleep for a few minutes and was awakened by the apartment door slamming shut. I got up to see what was going on and found lanky Arturo heading back to his room in boxer shorts. He and Ámbar had fought, and she'd left.

"She says I'm a real pain in the ass sometimes," said Arturo, who seemed very tense. "It's better that she's gone, Dad. I can't deal with any bullshit right now. I'll call her later to patch things up."

Twelve thirty-three.

I lay down next to Sara and heard Arturo, James, and Debrah talking quietly in the living room. Then they clattered in the kitchen as if they were making tea or coffee. The smell of tea wafted in. Then the smell of toast. I heard the noise of a knife scraping jam onto a piece of toast.

I placed my arm gently across Sara's breasts and squeezed her shoulder with my hand.

Caressing her, yes, and also seeking protection.

Twenty

I woke up in the grip of an attack of claustrophobia and had to struggle to bring it under control so I wouldn't start shrieking or who knows what. I sat up in bed, practically throwing off the blanket, and rushed to the window, where I breathed in deeply and looked out at the starry sky, the graves, and the trees. At about one in the morning, then, we had a skinny, naked man of almost sixty leaning out the window above a cemetery. But at least he wasn't shrieking.

Sara asked me what was going on, and I said, "Claustrophobia, but it's gone now. Lucky we've got these trees."

I smoked as I gazed down at the dark tombstones below. I went to the bathroom cabinet and took an extra antianxiety pill, clonazepam, which a doctor had prescribed a couple of months earlier.

"Should we call?"

"Let's let them rest."

Everybody was still in the kitchen. I went to get some tea, and as soon as Sara came in she asked Arturo about Ámbar. He said again that she'd left saying he was unbearable, but she was the one who was unbearable. Venus said it was better that way, that they'd get a break from each other, and Ámbar would be back. "I don't give a damn, as far as I'm concerned," Arturo said, too rudely and intensely for it to be true. I repeated, in English and because I didn't know what else to say, an old joke from Cali, "A woman who doesn't drive you crazy is a man," but only James found it funny.

The six of us sat down at the table to drink tea in silence. The atmosphere reminded me of a wake in Medellín fifty years ago. Through the window came an unpleasant squeal, maybe a squirrel being attacked by a rat or a rat being attacked by a squirrel down on the cemetery lawn. *The Garden of Earthly Delights*. Men with rat tails, marsupials with human legs. From the street also came the sound of a man and woman arguing, like a bundle of barbed wire. They were drunk, probably standing by the cemetery fence and very near one of the Virgins or the little bones of Ellen Louise Wallace, buried in 1975. We decided to call the boys.

Little bones.

To my surprise and perhaps to Ángela's, last week I asked her to buy me a bouquet of roses in the market square and go with me to visit Sara's grave. Old age astonishes me sometimes. I don't believe in the afterlife at all, nor that a corpse is anything but a muddle of calcium and tatters and disgusting but harmless insects, and look at me now with my silver-knobbed cane, a little pretentious, that I bought in an antique shop in

New York just because it was pretty, back when I didn't need it yet; the Basque beret the boys brought me; a black cotton blazer; dark-gray Levi's; brown suede shoes; a black leather belt with a simple silver buckle; my best shirt, buttoned up to the neck – that is, my full uniform for tossing myself off cliffs or receiving awards – standing before Sara's grave, where I just knelt to leave her a dozen yellow rose, their petals tipped with crimson. "I is someone else," a poet once said; he was French, but he said it as if he were Li Po. I didn't put on a tie because I didn't have one.

Later I'm going to try dictating to Ángela because my eyes are worn out again.

I had to go lie down a wile again because I couldn't sea anymore. I put a damp towl over my eyes to rest them. I was saying that at one in the morning we'd all gathered in the dinning room. We sat there mostly in silence, and evenchally decided to call the boys and all talk to them. First Debrah spoke, then James, cheering them up . . .

I loved Ángela's spelling. We can, when we least expect it, be so deeply moved by beauty! Of course at this point everything seems to move me, and I see (or sea) beauty everywhere I look. My older sister, who wrote like a dream, spelled badly too, garbling almost every word she set down. I think it's dyslexia. Ángela has nice handwriting too, but when I go back over the text to see where I am, little gems like evenchally, dinning, towl – and I don't call them gems sarcastically – inevitably distract me and make me lose the thread of my story. It's also complicated, for example, when she asks, "Dee what?" and I have to spell it out for her.

"D-e-b-r-a-h. Debrah. Capital *d*, *b* as in 'boy.' It's a name."

"With an *h* at the end?"

"Yes, Ángela."

"It's not Débora?"

I could dictate to her son, of course, who almost certainly spells better, but I don't want these, my personal matters, which are sometimes so difficult or intimate, to pass through the hairy hands of a male *Monkey sapiens*, especially not one as garrulous and chatty as him. To keep Ángela from being offended when I ceased to use her services, I explained to her as best I could that *e*-less towels made it hard for me to concentrate.

"As I see it, Don David," she answered, "a towel is still a towel, with or without an *e*."

I moved closer so I could look into her eyes and patted her cheek.

"Don't worry, Ángela, I'll put you to work writing again when I go totally blind."

I put on one of Bach's sonatas for violin and harpsichord, but played on the piano by Glenn Gould. I play the music on my computer, which my children set up for people with vision problems, so everything on the screen is huge and very high-contrast. Five in the afternoon. In an hour or so the bats will show up to flit around the edge of the eternal light. Let's leave the gathering in the dining room of the apartment on Second

Street, which is hard to write, for tomorrow. Ángela wasn't offended in the least and went to fetch me a strong coffee, which I requested so I could listen to the music better. Ángela is sturdy and short, not flabby, solid, strong, with large breasts and a beautiful face. Large, bright, black eyes. Very white skin, straight black hair. Very white teeth and an easy smile. Nude, she must look like a sort of Venus. I would have loved to do some charcoal sketches of her, even if she weren't nude.

Twenty-One

I talked to the boys last, but not in the dining room: instead, I went to the studio. And this time I was able to talk to Jacobo for a long time. He told me he was in a lot of pain but that at least he was feeling calmer. No, he couldn't sleep. This fucking pain won't let me get a wink. And now I'm constipated. I'm tired of needing help to take a shit, Dad. (My sons curse way more than I do.) Are you scared? I asked him baldly, and he said of course he was scared, David, do I look like Superman or something? I chuckled a bit, as if to comfort him. There was a long silence. It's okay if you change your mind, I said. I know, Dad, I know. It's okay if I change my mind. I said, you don't have to be strong or brave or anything, okay? Yes, David, I know, he said, seeming to grow impatient. How's Pablo? I asked. Good, he said. He's so huge he can carry the whole world and still have strength left over. Did you like the orchids he got done? he asked me. I did, I did, I said, but do you think he's going to get more tattoos? I think so, Dad, be prepared. Once they get started, they don't stop. But they look good, don't they? he asked. Beautiful, I told him. Hey, he said, and how do you think Mom's doing? I told him the truth: I think she'd rather you change your mind and come home, but I'm not positive about that either. Yeah, he said, we don't know anything. And how's it going with the ferry painting? he asked. It's right here in front of me. I haven't gotten it right yet, but I'm a little closer. Then I told him that Arturo had fought with his girlfriend and was very tense. Of course, David, no real surprise, with everything that's going on with me, right? Those last prints you did of Ámbar were fantastic, he said, quickly changing the subject. Yes, they turned out well, I told him, she's gorgeous. I hope they haven't broken up for good so I can do some more. Love you, Dad, he said in English, we'll talk soon. Love you too, Jacobo. Have Pablo give you a massage if it starts hurting a lot. And we'll be here. Take a couple of pain relievers, if only for the placebo effect, since I know they don't do anything for you, I said. Okay, David. Love you. Bye. Bye.

I remained with my elbows on my knees and my face in my hands, staring at the floor, sitting on the chair I used to study my paintings, in front of the light on the water that I still hadn't managed to capture. Sara came in and kissed the top of my head, my eyes, my nose, my mouth, and the top of my head again. It's a good thing it was only her, because in my fragile state I couldn't have endured another collective exhibition of grief à la USA.

And here the sentimental old man had to stop once more. Prostate. As if the world, thanks to my macular issues, hadn't become liquid enough already. I smoked a Pielroja, sitting on the edge of the bed, and lay down to sleep a while. I've never had prostate trouble, by the way. At my age I am proud that I still piss like a racehorse. I woke up maybe half an hour later feeling quite weak. Low blood pressure, maybe. Ángela brought me a large aguardiente, and the anise-flavored liquor revived me. I put on some Villa-Lobos, the same recording that helped me finally figure out the painting of the Staten Island ferry back then. And I sat down to my pages again with the magnifying glass, while the woman with a luminous voice sang a melody that I find funereal – *Bachiana Brasileira No. 5,* it's called, and I have no idea what the lyrics say because it's in Portuguese.

At six in the evening Ángela brought me my beer and said goodbye. It seemed like she wanted to say something else but couldn't work up the nerve. It's happened before, and I know she always ends up telling me about one of her family problems and asking my advice. I am quite fond of her and always resign myself to considering the problem and trying to suggest some reasonable solution, or at least one that seems reasonable to me. So I'll hear about it tomorrow or the day after at the latest.

I stayed on the porch in my sunflower-colored director's chair. Immense solitude is like a seemingly blank canvas, deceptively blank. At seven in the evening I went inside and shut the doors and windows, fumbling a little with the bolts and latches since my eyesight gets worse at night. I sat down in the leather armchair. Feeling a chill, I went to fetch the thick alpaca sweater that Sara gave me shortly before we left New York (comfortable, expensive, and beautiful, like all of her gifts). I sat down in the armchair again and remained motionless there for perhaps half an hour. Then a cricket began to sing beautifully, as if it were the presence of the Presence somewhere in the living room. These crickets are dark, nocturnal, ugly, vaguely reminiscent of cockroaches, and they have a powerful voice that not everyone enjoys. And my immense solitude was suddenly filled with the whole universe.

Twenty-Two

When Sara finished kissing my eyes and comforting me, it must have been two in the morning. That night nobody in the apartment would sleep, and only she and I would at some point make another attempt. I turned on the light above the painting and got to work; the others lingered around the kitchen table, chatting and drinking tea or black coffee. The telephone rang. I already knew who it was. I answered it.

"Good evening, Mr. David," said Michael O'Neal.

He apologized for calling so late and asked me if Venus was there. I told him she was. He asked to speak to her, if it wasn't too much trouble, and I called her. Venus thanked me, smiled, and went to Jacobo's room to talk to Michael O'Neal where I couldn't hear her. For a long time Venus had called me Mr. David, like Michael, until I finally persuaded her to call me by my first name pronounced in Spanish and without the "Mister." She was looking weary too.

"Do you want coffee?" asked Sara, who had come from the kitchen and was looking at the painting.

"I can't get the vertigo into it," I said.

She studied the painting a while longer.

"Don't be so sure," she said at last. "So do you want coffee or not?"

"Coffee, coffee, coffee," I said hastily to mask the intense rush of joy that must have shone in my eyes at her comment about the painting. It seemed absurd, almost obscene, to feel rushes of joy in our situation, but Sara wouldn't see it anyway, as she'd turned away and gone to get the coffee. When she brought it, she continued what she had been saying:

"And the foam is really looking beautiful now."

The foam had looked good from the beginning – I hadn't touched it again – but there was more contrast with the water now and it glowed more intensely. I have always put a lot of effort, a certain vehemence, into my work (though there has been no shortage of critics who call my art cold), but I was working away at this ferry painting as if all our lives depended on it. It was a battle against annihilation in which, to defeat chaos, I had to capture it in paint, like grabbing the devil by the tail and hurling him against a wall. And here the religious images from my childhood in the ultra-Catholic town of Envigado reappear, somewhat transformed, and absurdly associated with a nearly abstract painting that only a moron could find cold.

Venus came and told me that Michael knew about Jacobo and was very interested, as he intended to go the same route if everything went well today. Jacobo was ten years older than Michael, and Michael idolized him. My son loved him dearly and sincerely praised him for his extensive medical knowledge – specializing, of course, in his own condition – which was unusual in someone so young and self-taught. The thing is, he literally learned it in the flesh, poor boy, and that helped.

Venus looked beautiful in the lamplight that illuminated the painting, with the sober but not tearful expression of sadness that you see on people who are used to facing pain daily and deeply. Once more I thought of the funeral portraits of the women in the Roman colonies in Egypt and of the melancholy of death that appears in some of them.

"It is fucking hard," she said in English.

"Sí. Fucking hard," I said, though I never curse.

Without my asking, Venus went to the kitchen, brought me a coffee, and set it on the little table beside the painting, which she eyed with evident admiration and without saying anything. Two thirty in the morning. It is amazing how a painting can change so much with just a few brushstrokes, in less than five minutes. The struggle is not so much with the paintbrush as with the eye, with the doors of perception, which resist opening even a crack.

Laughter came from the living room. Arturo was probably clowning around. That weedy kid did a perfect impression of Preet talking with me, and he played both roles: when he was Preet, Arturo went to the taxi driver's favorite armchair, moving quickly to my chair when it came time to play my part.

"Sikhism has its origins in the fifteenth century," Arturo lilted in an exaggerated Punjabi accent, and then flew to sit in my chair, one leg draped over the other. He is already tall and skinny to start with, but somehow he seemed to become even more tall and skinny, and above all more stoic.

"Is that so? How remarkable."

Arturo knew how to create the extended pause that always followed. Then he rushed to Preet's chair.

"The term *sikh* comes from the Sanskrit word *sişya*, which means 'disciple, student,' or from *śikşa*, which means 'teaching.' We Sikhs are disciples of the guru."

Another dash to my seat.

"Incredible. Incredible. Isn't it, Sara?" said Arturo in my precise but heavily accented English. My desperate attempts to make Preet leave me alone and talk to her instead were quite comical.

When Arturo was finished goofing around, we drank more tea and more coffee and sat in silence. A shadow suddenly came over Sara's face, and she hastily went to our room, where we wouldn't see her. No one went to comfort her. We knew full well that it wasn't possible, and that she wanted to be alone.

Twenty-Three

Last night before I fell asleep I was thinking that I'd like to experience some real hot weather and decided we should go to Girardot today, the city I mentioned earlier that is dilapidated, sweltering, and still lovely on the banks of the Magdalena River. And here I am in the hotel room at six thirty in the afternoon on July 6, 2018, writing a few lines at the desk, to which I've clamped my jointed-arm magnifying glass. I have the window open, the lowland crickets are chirping, and I can smell the thick scent of vegetation, which always makes me happy. I feel so happy sometimes! Now I'm going to stop writing and go out to smoke a Pielroja at one of the tables beside that gorgeous swimming pool, and drink a cold beer, or maybe two.

Ten in the morning. I had my cold beer last night, two of them, and two glasses of aguardiente and a glass of wine, and today I'm feeling the hangover even though I ate grilled pork loin, which they do well here at the hotel, before I went to bed. But no sadness. I didn't manage to persuade Ángela to get in the pool. I never have, but this time she decided to buy a bathing suit in one of the local department stores. And her embarrassment, I think, is not at revealing her body but at getting into a pool for rich people. I wanted to see her in a bathing suit in the sun. I am still perhaps too eager to admire all the world's forms, even though they look wavering and rather liquid to me. When we were driving down, crossing the bridge we saw that the Magdalena was almost dry, and the wide, deep riverbed, with rowboats and ships stranded in the sand, though I had difficulty seeing it, reminded me of those paintings from the whatever-teenth century in which the landscape of a river or bay, sometimes with buildings or ruins of buildings, looks like something out of a dream or a nightmare. But because my eyesight is so bad, the images I form now seem to come as much from within me as from without, and sometimes I can't tell if I'm seeing what I see, or creating it, or remembering it, or imagining it . . .

Sara had gone to the bedroom to be alone in her sadness. I too, sitting in front of the painting again but not looking at it, looking at the floor, had been gripped powerfully by sorrow again, and the flames licked at me from within, sometimes on one side and sometimes on the other, nearly suffocating me. With all my soul I wanted Jacobo to come home, even if only years of suffering awaited him. I went to the bedroom and lay down on Sara's side of the bed. She was in the bathroom washing her face. I closed my eyes to contemplate the flames. Sara came out not long after and lay down behind me, gently pressing against my body, almost floating like a cloud. She put her hand on mine, and the two of them formed a snail shell on my leg.

As the seconds passed, reality became more intense. Sara's hand was a little cold but grew gradually warmer. I felt irregularities in my heart, little skips and murmurs and also oddly powerful heartbeats that shook my body imperceptibly. "I can't die right now," I thought. "What would happen to them?" I started to breathe more deeply and regularly, until the murmuring and hammering stopped. But not the flames. "I can't go falling apart all the time like a crazy person, especially not right now," I thought, and managed to pull myself together. I thought about the Irishman who painted screaming popes. Time was passing very slowly, almost turning back on itself, but only to crush us more thoroughly and lick us better with its flames. The insidious silence settled back over the apartment even though Debrah and James were talking in the kitchen and Arturo was playing his guitar in his bedroom, and despite the usual sounds of breaking bottles of the Lower East Side and the shouts that occasionally drifted in, as if from very far away . . .

"Hey! Fucking bitch!" they shouted.

Last week I talked to Debrah and James. They got spots in an old folks' home on Long Island that has a golf course, pool, and bowling alley. They described it to me as if they considered it heaven on earth, and the more facilities they mentioned, the more on-call nurses and doctors twenty-four hours a day they mentioned, the more appalling it seemed to me. Of course I congratulated them, though I couldn't help saying it wasn't my sort of thing. James went quiet for a moment, and I was sorry I'd said it. I asked when they were moving, and he said they'd move out of one of the studios in a month and a half. James's voice is rich and warm, and it has gotten even richer and warmer with age. More musical, if you like, as if it hadn't been musical enough already. Debrah's voice, on the other hand, has become slightly high-pitched and impertinent – that is, she has a fitting voice for the brilliant, tiny, inquisitive woman she still is today.

Twenty-Four

In the afternoon Ángela decided to get in the pool. Though I couldn't see her well, I knew she was striding toward the water with her gleaming white teeth, short, broad, sturdy, perfectly proportioned for her personality. I didn't want to ask her to come closer so I could see her better because I thought she might think I was being a dirty old man. The bathing suit was a black one-piece with orange polka dots about two centimeters in diameter. Her beautiful white-and-coral skin glowed with health in the sun. Her skin had that touch of blue that sclerotic infants have. The "squintier" I get, the more detail-oriented I become. Because Sara wasn't there to warn her to put on sunblock, I had to do it.

And, to my surprise, she knew how to swim. I went to the edge of the pool, with my cane, with my shorts, with my bare saggy chest, with my flip-flops, my straw hat, my long, skinny legs, and I saw her swimming, and again I was moved. She swam beautifully. Not a crawl but a breaststroke, hardly moving the water at all, like an aquatic animal.

"Where did you learn to swim, Ángela?" I asked her when she emerged from the pool and came to sit across from me at the table.

A waiter approached and asked us if we wanted anything ("desire," he said). I ordered a Coke.

"And for you, madam?"

You could see Ángela was pleased by the waiter's deference, and she ordered a Coke too.

I'm going to forget about the whole Jacobo business while we're here. Tomorrow, when we go back home, I'll keep going with it, which demands all five of my senses and occasionally overwhelms me entirely.

Ángela said she'd learned to swim in the Cauca River, since she'd grown up in Cártago. "Big and ugly, like Cártago" is what we Colombians say to describe things that are . . . big and ugly – a car, say, or a horse – but I don't know if it's accurate with regard to Cártago itself, as I have only a vague recollection of the city. I do recall that it's large in comparison with the neighboring villages, but I don't remember it as being particularly ugly.

"My dad would take us to the river, tie a rope around our waist, and toss us into the water."

"That's why you swim with your head up out of the water, to keep an eye out for tree trunks coming downstream."

"Is that why?"

Ángela was quiet a while, idly watching people go in and out of the pool but with her mind on other things. I realized what was coming. And sure enough, a little later she asked me whether she could consult me about a personal matter. Boom, boom, one surprise after another. It turns out her husband is having an affair with a young woman who works on a fern plantation near Ángela's house. "A trifer farm," she called it, using the local term for a feathery variety of fern, apparently a close relative of the asparagus, known in English as a *trifern*. And Ángela, who isn't exactly in love with her husband from what I can tell, doesn't know what to do. Really, she's more confused than angry about the whole thing. She told me the other little details of the situation, and I told her I'd think about it and offer my advice.

Sara would have settled the matter in no time. But I didn't feel comfortable asking "What about you, Ángela – do you love him?" It would have sounded odd coming from an old man like me, and I think it would have made even me laugh. And for country people, or maybe for everybody, love with all its intensity works for a while, when people are young, but it eventually loses its meaning as it becomes clear that a couple's relationship is a question of survival and can always be summed up this way: "To keep the earth from swallowing us, you go out and swing a hoe, and I'll cook and take care of the kids." Love: irrelevant.

That's the tangle I'm in.

Twenty-Five

Lying next to Sara, our hands still curled on my leg, I thought how all of us – Sara, me, the three boys, James, Debrah, Venus, and Michael O'Neal – seemed to be locked for eternity in a burning house. Sometimes I opened my eyes and saw the blind night through the window; I closed them again and contemplated the grief devouring me from within like the burning bush.

Sara's phone rang, and I bolted upright like a spring. Instead of answering, she embraced me and soothed me. Then she returned the boys' call, and it went the same as it always did. "Yes, yes, yes, of course," said Sara, walking toward the bathroom. "I understand. But you have to do things . . . What? Exactly. Yes, exactly. Yes, yes, yes," she said. She went into the bathroom and the awful lullaby cadence began, while I fled to the living room window to try to breathe the unwalled air and look at the Virgins below or to close my eyes and contemplate the burning bush inside me. I didn't know how much time had passed, or which way it was going, or whether I'd fallen asleep at the window or maybe lost consciousness for a few seconds. Time was moving forward and backward, like a pendulum or like a reaper. Then I felt Sara's breasts pressing against my back. (When she reached menopause, Sara said, "I'm not going let my parts dry up like pumice stone. I don't care if I get cancer, I'm taking hormones." She began hormone replacement therapy, and her parts never dried up, or anything close.)

"Are you okay?" she asked.

"What did they say?"

"It's fine. Everything's fine," she said after a while, and I didn't ask anything further so as not to risk losing hope.

We didn't go back to bed. Sara went to talk with Debrah and James in the kitchen, and I went to take another antianxiety pill, which seemed to have an effect this time, and then to the studio to examine the painting. It was already very close to the abyss. The problem, it seemed to me, didn't have to do with the luminous side of light; I was avoiding its other side.

Sara came back and suggested I go out for a bit. I had stashed my wristwatch deep in a drawer so I wouldn't be looking at it every ten seconds, and I asked her what time it was. She told me it was three. Three! There's still time, I thought, and Sara realized what was going through my mind, looked at me compassionately, and insisted I go out for a bit to get some air.

I walked down First Avenue to St. Mark's Place, and from there to

Astor Place. I didn't want hard liquor, only a beer, so I bought a large bottle of Beck's in one of those twenty-four-hour corner stores, which they gave to me, as always, in a brown paper bag. A city bus passed; there were only two people on it, like two seahorses in a lighted fish tank (though the image also evoked that melancholy painter from Nyack whose name I never manage to remember).

I sat at the foot of the cube sculpture to drink my beer. Two young men were doing spins on their skateboards. They moved without speaking, and the sound of skateboards and rollerblades echoed in the night. (Hopper! That's the name of the painter from Nyack.) I looked up, looking for the stars, and there they were. Only someone without air, like me, would look for stars in Astor Place, outside Starbucks and Kmart. But I didn't get to look at them long because a man about my age approached with a bicycle loaded with a basket full of some fifty vinyl records.

As things always are in New York, it was complicated.

The man's name was Anthony and he spoke English with a heavy foreign accent. It turned out he was from Russia and had been in the United States for ten years, but he didn't consider himself Russian, despite the accent, and he didn't like speaking Russian, because he thought of himself as an American. He had lived in Rio for four years and also spoke Portuguese. He spoke to me in Portuguese for a while, and I asked him to switch to English, please, as I didn't speak Portuguese.

I cursed the bad luck that had put me in this mess, which could only happen in New York, right when I didn't have the strength to deal with it. I knew these messes all too well, and I knew that things tended to get complicated.

Anthony bought and sold vinyl records. Without my asking, he took the fifty records from his basket and spread them out in front of the cube sculpture like a carpet, then sat down beside me to gaze at them. There was no way to look at the stars. The skateboards rumbled on the pavement. Anthony wasn't leaving me any time to think about Jacobo either.

"Rolling Stones," he said, pointing to a record in a nearby corner of the carpet, and indeed there it was, the donkey with the drums and the man dressed in white leaping with two guitars.

"Hm!" I said, unable to think of anything else to say.

Anthony remained quiet for a long time, but that was even worse, leaving me even more trapped than I would have been if he'd chattered incessantly. I liked him, too, and I was already intrigued.

I offered him the bottle.

"Okay," he said and took a swig. I wiped the mouth of the bottle with my shirt, took a swig, and so it was established that we would drink the beer together. A bad time to make friends, I thought, but what are you going to do – you live in the city you live in. Someone went by and the flash of a camera illuminated us and blinded us there by the records. A fraction of a second later, Starbucks, Kmart, and the records appeared again. I asked Anthony his last name and he said his name was Anton and something that sounded like it ended in *insky*.

"Kandinsky?" I asked, and he smiled.

"No. Anton Demidovsky, but people call me Stravinsky because of the music," he explained, and gestured toward the Rolling Stones' donkey.

Twenty-Six

I lay down a moment to rest, and immediately heard Ángela knocking on the door. I got up to open it and told her to sit down. I'd thought about the situation with her husband and his fern girl, and maybe I had a solution.

"Whose name is the farm in, Ángela?" I asked. She was unfazed by the pragmatic coarseness of the question.

"The farm is mine."

"All right, then," I said, relieved. "There's not much to think about. You tell him that he has to either dump the girl or get out. You don't need him for anything, right?"

"Well, no. The kids are all grown up."

I seemed to be confirming what she herself had already decided. I almost said "Easy-peasy," but I refrained. Ángela stood there in the half-shadow of the room, all lovely and solid, pondering with an intensity and seriousness reminiscent of a precocious child. I didn't want to tell her that he was no dummy and wasn't going to run off with the mistress, because I might be wrong about that.

"Yes," Ángela said at last. "The kids are grown. Would you like a coffee?"

I told her I would, yes, and she went to fetch it and I returned to my desk. I put on a concerto for piccolo and strings and basso continuo, which seems like it was written for blue-and-gray tanagers, and of course I couldn't work, distracted by the intricate weaving of the little flute. "That music you play is like Semana Santa music, but very pretty," Ángela always says. Which is not true. I play Miles Davis sometimes; Bechet, the slow pieces; Pee Wee Russell; Django Reinhardt; and also music in Spanish: Amanda Miguel, Lucho Gatica, or the rancheras of Chavela Vargas when she was young and didn't caterwaul the way she did as an old woman. Singers, boxers, womanizers, bullfighters, and football players who grow long in the tooth and refuse to retire are always pathetic. And that's coming from me, whom old age has left or is going to leave as blind as a baby parrot and who had to give up his much-loved craft and resign himself to writing. And who knows how much longer I'll be able to keep setting my affairs down on these pages.

Ángela brought the coffee, and just as she was setting it on the table, the landline rang. That always means trouble, I said, and asked her to go answer it in the kitchen. She came back a minute later. It was as I'd guessed.

"If the journalist is old, tell him I've got Alzheimer's but that I some-times have good days and he should call back."

"But you don't have Alzheimer's, Don David."

"Ángela!"

"Ohhh, okay, okay. She's young, I think. A woman."

"You're sure she's a she?" I asked, and Ángela laughed and bright-ened as I'd hoped.

She was young, her name was Flor or Fleur, and she had a French accent. They wanted to make a documentary on three Latin American visual artists, and I was one of them. "The main one," she said, and that bugged me, how people are obsessed with establishing hierarchies that always end up corrupting artists. "So the other two are second-rank artists, then?" I asked to trip her up a little. She stammered, gave me the two names – two other prostates – stammered a little more, and finally laughed. "For France?" I asked for the heck of it, as I have no preference with regard to countries or continents. Yes, she said, Paris. "And why not one painter from Japan, one from Morocco, and another from the Netherlands?" I asked. She had regained her footing by now and replied that she thought it was a wonderful idea and would propose it as soon as she'd finished this project. I told her to come visit me and we'd see.

Twenty-Seven

Two young men walked by with a pit bull that seemed anything but aggressive. Healthy, tattooed, they reminded me of Pablo. A world without suffering, I thought, would be as incomplete and as inharmonious, as ugly, as a sculpture or a tree that had no shadow. And there I was – suffocation, confinement – at the foot of the Astor Place cube, next to some guy named Anthony and several dozen records in the glow of a streetlamp.

But it turns out it's easy to accept pain when it's not your own, and my son's pain was definitely mine. As I talked to Anthony – and suffered – I understood a little better the expression on Jacobo's face when he tried to be social, to be with people in the living room, while pain racked his legs or abdomen. He spoke very little at times like those because of the agony; he smiled sometimes, and visible in that smile were the grimace and glittering tears of pain that were always on the verge of spilling out.

My eldest son.

Anthony told me, as the flames licked at the back of my eyes and the base of my skull, that he made his living buying and selling those records, some of which were gems. The bicycle was the only thing he needed for his work, and the basket. What was amazing was that he had traveled all over the world buying records and coming back to sell them in New York. He had customers on Madison Avenue, on Fifth, on Park. He had been in Bogotá, he said. He had been in Bombay. In Havana. The best city was São Paulo, a treasure trove of rare vinyl in good condition. In other words, I said, distracted from my sorrows, the tools of your trade are the bicycle, the bike basket, and a jet. He laughed, pleased with himself – quite impressed with himself, really – and asked for another swig of beer. He finished off the bottle and went to buy two more.

"Something's wrong, isn't it?" he asked after a while.

A man with a strong Medellín accent then explained to a man with a strong Russian accent – in other words, two quintessential New Yorkers – what had happened, what was happening, and what was almost certainly going to happen with Jacobo, his eldest son, twenty-eight years old. Anthony didn't try to hug me or pat me on the back to comfort me or anything like that. He only said, "Oh, man!" The people of New York are a reserved bunch. They have big hearts, but they don't sniffle or act like sentimental fools, at least not in public. And so you can be one of two ways in the city: either with your composure carefully under control, or totally schizoid and babbling to yourself or to phantasms along the bridges and avenues.

After that, Stravinsky and I talked about other things or just sat in silence. "Oh, man!" he said quietly another couple of times, as if he were still thinking about Jacobo. A group of dirty, smelly young men and women in dark clothing had gathered on the Fourth Avenue side of the square. They played their guitars badly, played their flutes badly, played their drums badly. They had rings in their noses and were sitting next to large, dirty black backpacks. When the breeze picked up, the smell of old sweat drifted over us. At about three thirty in the morning we finally did hug – to say goodbye – and each of us continued on his way in the ocean of the New York night . . .

I would love for Sara to be here so she could tell me, "David, that last bit was so cheesy, it makes me want to kiss you." She sometimes said things like that, not always. Only when she knew they'd throw me off.

So scratch the bit about the ocean of New York. I went back down Lafayette and Bleecker so I didn't have to walk past the odoriferous panhandling kids. On Second I crossed La Salle and paused at the corner of the cemetery to look up at the windows of the apartment. The light, framed and flurried by the metallic shadow of the ivy climbing up from the cemetery, looked cozy, as if the place did not know suffering. I looked at the grave.

Ellen Louise Wallace, 1880–1975. Ninety-five years old when she returned to the void.

I opened the front door of the building and Ámbar appeared out of nowhere. She smiled in greeting and asked after Arturo. I told her to come up, that Arturo was fine, he was upstairs. Ámbar must have gone home, because everything she was wearing, except her jewelry, was different from what she'd had on a few hours earlier, including her makeup. She was wearing a light-pink shirt, dark-green harem pants, and clear orange plastic sandals. A little West Village vampire. And it occurs to me, as I think back on climbing those poorly lit stairs, that if she'd started flying, she would have flown like the bats in La Mesa, which look like butterflies.

"Ámbar, what time is it?"

She said it was five past five. Are you sure? I almost asked her. It was as if words were no longer able to contain time, nor I to understand it, nor clocks to measure it.

Twenty-Eight

Ángela's husband is named José Luis, or maybe Juan Pablo, and her son is named Juan Pablo, or maybe José Luis, or Juan José.

"Tell Juan Pablo to please come by here tomorrow to take me to the notary office" – I'm just giving this as an example, since the notary office is only three blocks away, but I don't have time to come up with a more plausible scenario.

"It's José Luis, Don David. Juan Pablo is my husband."

Sometimes I call them Juan Luis, Luis Pablo, and other combinations, and it's a rare occasion when I actually get it right and no one has to correct me.

What's in a name?

Ángela's son is talkative, yes, but funny, and he's an excellent driver. He once told me a story about seeing two farmers, father and son, probably, in a pasture near a town called Funza, wielding ropes and chasing a very large, unfriendly cow, one of those lanky Holsteins you see on the damp plateau outside Bogotá. They reached a fence and the cow leaped it effortlessly, as if it had wings, leaving the farmers on the other side of the five strands of barbed wire, watching its rump disappear into the distance and then looking at each other, their ropes dangling from their hands. Everything Ángela's son recounts creates an image. If you picked up a pencil and paper, you could draw his stories as he tells them. They are always a little absurd, comical, and he hardly ever needs to repeat one because he has so many: he keeps his eyes open and is good at observing the world.

Ángela's son is quite fond of our station wagon. I think he wouldn't have been able to bear seeing Sara load it with mossy stones or bags of plants, or the endless bales of manure that she went out to buy from nearby farms to keep the garden lush. When we got back from Girardot at about four in the afternoon, the first thing he did was go wash it down with soap and vacuum the mats and seats. Juan Pablo, or José Luis, or Juan José takes care of it as if it were a living animal, a fine mare or a dairy cow.

Holstein.

At six I was perched in my yellow chair again with my beer in my hand, waiting for the bats. And they came, of course, or I thought I saw them come, which is the same thing. It's funny because now they remind me of Ámbar, Arturo's girlfriend, because of what I said about how she could have leaped into flight as we climbed the poorly lit stairs to the apartment.

Words are amazing things. I already tried my hand at poetry and short stories when I was very young, and I didn't do so badly. In those days I seemed to have more aptitude for that than I did for painting: it was in my blood, since some members of my family had been writers. And now that I'm back at it all these years later, I am surprised once more by how supple words are – how all by themselves, or practically by themselves, they can express the ambiguity, the changeability, the fickleness of things. They are like the world: unstable as a house in flames, as a burning bush. And yet I long for the aroma of oils or the powdery feel of charcoal in my fingers, and I miss the pang – like the pang of love – that you feel when you sense you have touched infinity, captured an elusive light, a difficult light, with a bit of oil mixed with ground-up metals or stones.

I believe at one point I said words are a clumsy medium, and here I am saying they're supple. Both things are true. It all depends whether they feel like being clumsy or deign to be supple.

Sara was waiting for me at the apartment door. I looked into her eyes to see whether there was any word from Portland. Cristóbal twined around my legs. Sara shook her head, welcoming Ámbar with a hug and complimenting her on her outfit. Old beanpole Arturo slunk out of his room and hugged her too. Ámbar's eyelids, made up in olive green with a black border, hit the kid at his sternum.

Twenty-Nine

This morning I stayed under the electric blanket the boys brought me longer than usual. I'm not depressed – quite the opposite: everything felt so good there in bed, I was so centered in the world, so at peace, that getting up would have been ridiculous. I recalled the serenity of one of my maternal great-aunts who died at ninety-five (like Ellen Louise Wallace) when she'd stay in bed till nine in the morning or even later, looking at the world with her liquid, blue, tranquil eyes. As a boy I was always amazed by the old woman's peacefulness; as an adult I forgot about it entirely; and now, suddenly, I don't just remember that peace and stillness, I understand it – and I don't just understand it, I share it.

And – words are amazing things – through a bit of sorcery Ellen Louise Wallace turned into my great-aunt Antonia Latorre Estrada, my grandmother Natalia's spinster sister who always lived with her, and who crocheted and read books and smoked Pielrojas, and who loved us.

I had two great-aunts who were the yin and yang of great-aunts:

Antonia, on my mother's side, and cruel Pepa, on my father's side, who called her blind nieces "squinty." Sheer coincidence. Nothing to do with the character of the two sides of the family.

"Is everything okay, Don David?" asked Ángela when she came in at nine thirty to retrieve the mug of coffee she'd placed on my nightstand at seven, and brought me another.

"Yes, Ángela. Leave it on the desk, all right? I'm heading there in a minute."

"All right. The blankets had you pinned down or something?"

"Sure did."

"How many spoonfuls of sugar?"

"One. Same as always."

"You're sure you're all right?"

"I'm fine, Ángela. Don't be a nag."

"Mr. Persnickety."

I stayed in bed a while longer and finally got up so the coffee wouldn't get cold. I turned on the desk lamp, adjusted the magnifying glass, straightened my papers, dipped my pen in the inkpot, and filled the reservoir with blackberry-colored ink. Nineteen years earlier, in 1999, I'd come back from talking with Anthony Stravinsky on Astor Place, entered the apartment, and gone to the bathroom to take a crap and another half-tablet of clonazepam. Everybody had apparently gotten worried when I took so long out on the street, and now they were all gathered in the dining room again.

I came back from the bathroom and encountered the kind of silence that falls when people have been talking about you. I'd glanced in the mirror, and I was definitely looking haggard, but I had no intention of shaving at five thirty in the morning, nor was anyone asking me to. Arturo and Ámbar were playing some complicated game with their hands that had to do with guessing which finger was going to move the other; it might have been of their own invention, and even they didn't seem to understand the rules very well. Several times he put his hands on the table with his palms facing up, and she'd rest her fingertips on his. When the turn was over, they'd switch positions. They played in silence, listlessly. Ámbar, who had long, slender hands, called him a cheater and suddenly quit playing. Debrah, Venus, and James had been intrigued, of course, as had Sara and I, though only idly, and not enough to ask the kids for any sort of explanation.

Arturo was twenty-four now, and Ámbar was eighteen, and they seemed to be tarrying a bit in adolescence still. In a way, I was happy about that, as I'd never seen the appeal – still don't, in fact – of becoming serious and responsible. Nor did Sara. After finishing high school at nineteen, Arturo took a year off and traveled to Machu Picchu, Thailand, and other places. He came back and took another year off to tour the United

States with a rock band. He came back again and went to college to study art, and that's what he was doing when he started dating Ámbar. She had a vague plan to study in one of New York's many design schools.

Pablo, on the other hand, who had decided to take care of Jacobo from the beginning, had always been more serious and responsible, and he hadn't seen much of the world. He found freedom in his beautiful tattoos and his camera lens out on the streets. He'd had a lot of girl-friends, or none, and sometimes he brought them home and introduced them to us, but none of them had lasted, for no particular reason. Pablo, as was often the case with the protagonists of the romance novels that my Great-Aunt Antonia so loved reading – and which I read too, as a boy, because she lent them to me – still hadn't found the person who was meant for him, his soul mate, the love of his life.

Thirty

"Lunch is ready, Mr. Persnickety. Don't ignore it too," Ángela said from the doorway, and I turned off the light and closed my eyes to rest them a few seconds. I opened them and looked out the window at the blurry purple of the flowers on the bougainvillea vine that frames it. Everything shimmered, went hazy or liquid. "It's going to get cold," Ángela said.

Lunch, nap, coffee. I accompanied Ángela to a bakery where they sell the best caramel jam in the country, ten blocks from here. We passed the church, with its oddly wide-spaced spires, and Ángela went in to pray for a minute while I waited on a bench outside, my chin resting on the knob of my cane. Ángela returned. We walked down a narrow street undulating with vans and cars, the world liquid, like a tank of clear oil. Home. I rested in bed a few minutes. I can't go out for even a short walk without needing a nap afterward.

Magnifying glass.

Then Michael O'Neal called and talked to Sara. I was making myself some coffee. My eyelids were heavy and my eyes were burning. "Yes, sweetie," she was saying. Sara's English was heavily accented with the Cauca Valley, the way mine is accented with Medellín, but hers, while it might have been less correct than my own, was much more fluid, effective, and expressive. Here what she said to Michael: "Six their time, nine here. Yes, sweetie. Of course, yes. I think calm, I think. What did you say? Yes, yes, yes, yes. He is coming, yes, at six their time, that seems definite. Oh, Michael, sweetie," said Sara, and her voice cracked. "Yes, yes, yes. Hugs to you too. We'll call you. Yes."

Not the burning bush, which burned without being consumed. And I was being consumed. I drank the coffee and went to fetch the other half-tablet of clonazepam, as confinement and suffocation were bearing down on me again. Sara asked me if I was okay and I said I was okay. She asked again if I was sure I was okay, but I didn't tell her not to be a nag the way I did Ángela this morning, though I came close. Instead I told her I was okay, and she sensed the hint of impatience in my voice and left me alone.

"Bring Mr. Persnickety another cup of coffee, would you?" I said to Ángela a little while ago, by way of apology for my grumpy mood this morning, and she pretended not to forgive me, her expression stern. A moment later she reappeared with the coffee, smiling.

There have been some major developments on that front. Just as I predicted, Ángela's husband ran off with the fern girl. Ángela doesn't know where the two of them are living, and she doesn't much care. But

126

that's not the news. The news is that he keeps coming to work in the garden and she keeps serving him breakfast, lunch, and dinner, as a worker now, but they don't speak to each other. At first they tried to use me as a go-between and I flatly refused. Leave notes for each other, work it out however you wish, but don't stick me in the middle of this, I said. Just picture an elderly gentleman of seventy-eight like me telling another woman's ex-husband, "See here, José Luis, Ángela wants to tell you breakfast is ready."

And the ex-husband replying, "It's Juan Pablo, Don David. José Luis is my son. Thank you very much. Please tell her I'm on my way."

"Ángela, Juan Luis is on his way."

"Thank you, Don David. Who?"

That bit was pretty funny, Sara would have said. *Not sidesplitting, mind you. But amusing.*

I'm a serious person but, as I understand it – and I hope I'm not mistaken – I have a sense of humor. I know this because at one point I used to write letters, many letters, to anyone who would read them. People said they were funny, and it must be true, because I had fun writing them. That's why I wrote them, really. Sara received a lot of my correspondence, poor thing. Sometimes I'd leave the letter on her desk and wait in my studio with my ears pricked to hear if she laughed. And she said they were lovely, my letters, despite my tendency to get deep sometimes, or to complain about being down in the dumps.

At the moment, despite the events I'm describing, or perhaps because of them, I see that on the whole I'm enjoying myself. The truth is that it's been a long time since all that – nineteen years – and only in certain instants does the pain in my heart stab me as it did back then; only occasionally do I feel the flames and the devastation as acutely as I did in those days. I am still crushed by what happened, of course, and it makes me smoke cigarettes and take naps, because it was tough, but joy always, or almost always, sprouts like a piece of wood in water, no matter the depth of the horror a person has experienced.

And the whole Ángela situation made me realize that, at my age, when you're hungry you don't need to be called. When the hour approaches, the ex-husband gradually moves to a strategic distance from the table on the back porch where she serves him his meals, diligently weeding or hoeing while keeping a constant eye on the table. Ángela could torture him and dawdle ten or fifteen minutes till Juan Pablo's stomach is growling, or serve him half an hour early, when he's not paying attention, so the soup goes cold and bugs fly into it, but she doesn't. She's too professional to stoop to such manipulations. She serves right on time and leaves, and he slinks over to the table. We humans are monkeys with a million little tricks.

Thirty-One

Sara finished talking to Michael and remained there a while, sitting across from me in the living room, without saying anything. The Earth's gravitational pull had increased.

"I met a former Russian who makes his living selling records to customers on Fifth Avenue and Park Avenue," I told her to distract her. "They call him the Stravinsky of Vinyl."

I told her about his travels.

"Do you think it's true?" Sara asked.

"I don't know, I think so. It's too complicated to have made it all up, don't you think?"

"Do you think he'll change his mind?"

I didn't know whether she wanted Jacobo to change his mind or not.

"I don't think so," I told her, though I did know what I wanted.

At daybreak, fatigue overwhelmed me. I lay down on the bed for a moment and woke up at ten. The sun was pouring through the windows that looked out on cemetery. Cristóbal, stretched out on the sill, was glowing.

It had been a long time since I'd seen sunlight.

In life, major events mix together with minor ones, and after a long time has passed, perspectives are lost. Nobody knows what is minor, what is major. Nobody knows if there are things that are less important than others. Nobody knows if things have some kind of order or if they are arbitrary. Right now, for example, the most important thing is that the fern girl is making Ángela's ex-husband's life miserable. She just told me about it. His suffering began practically the next day after they started living together. She's cheating on him, she's taking his money, she mocks him in public, she makes him do the housekeeping, she doesn't feed him, and she won't sleep with him.

Ángela and I smile at each other.

We went to Bogotá again on Saturday, to the eye doctor. There's nothing to be done. The doctor doesn't know anything about anything. Hardly any patients with macular degeneration end up blind. Except me. I won't go totally blind, as I think I already said: I'll still see light and some shadows and forms. But anyway. We went to lunch. There downtown I felt the movement of the city, the pulse, as they call it. We went to the Parque Nacional to be around people and eat roasted corn on the cob, which I have a hard time chewing these days but have loved as long as I can remember. We sat on a sunny bench and Ángela's son told me the story of the time he was going along a dirt road and came across a man carrying a large quantity of weapons. "He had pistols, revolvers, even submachine guns, Don David." Ángela's son said he kept going and five minutes later came across another man carrying even more weapons than the first. Ángela's son has a knack for the absurd, that's what he likes, and he lets images hang in the air a while, like a vision or the tolling of a bell. Ten minutes later he came upon people taking apart the filming gear for a gunfight scene for the soap opera *The Chestnut Filly*, which takes place in a pasture. Ángela's son always pays close attention to things, so he must have stopped to ask the production crew the name of the soap opera, and he may have even asked them to describe the episode, but if that's how it happened, he didn't tell me that part.

This is the last time I'll be coming to the eye doctor. It's the last time I'll eat roasted corn and sit in the sun in the Parque Nacional. Many things will forever be illuminated in my heart: this park; Central Park; the Botanical Garden in Brooklyn; the sea at Coney Island; the light in La Guajira on the Caribbean coast; the light in Islamorada, in the Keys; the light in Medellín during my boyhood; the mountains east of Bogotá; the sea by the Cape Florida Lighthouse in Miami, before the hurricane uprooted the lovely Australian pines that grew there; the cormorants that perched in those pines; Sara's smile; Venus's smile and the smiles of her children; the schools of green fish in the East River; Jacobo's shining, intelligent eyes; James's musical voice; all of Debrah (she's small); the tattoos of Pablo, our illustrated giant, stable as a rock; and Arturo's long fingers, so similar to mine.

All of that, in minute detail, here with me.

Thirty-Two

Cristóbal glowed in the sun on the windowsill as if he were being stroked by the hand of God. I went to the living room and knew just from looking at Sara that Jacobo had died. I felt a sharp pain in the pit of my stomach, a rush of nausea, and saw a reddish shimmer. When I regained consciousness a few minutes later, I was sitting on the sofa with Sara beside me. Cristóbal had moved to the living room window and was still there, full of light.

Just then I realized that everyone was there. I looked at the line that sun was tracing, sharp as a knife, across the floorboards.

"What about Pablo?"

"He's already on the plane," Sara told me.

Now we had to wait for them to call us and go to retrieve Jacobo. The four of us would go to Portland. Pablo would have to make the trip again. The blade of sun on the floor was moving imperceptibly, and the luminous rectangle was shrinking on the hardwood. Cristóbal jumped down from the window to the floor and walked with his light toward Arturo's room, like a beacon.

We talked in the living room, and then in the dining room, about practical, specific things. We talked about how there was the remote possibility that we would get into legal trouble and what the best thing to do would be in that case. We talked about the logistics of death: the cremation process, the cost. We would use Díaz Funeral Home on Second Street, and the ceremony would be small and quick, just as Jacobo had wanted it.

Luckily nobody said his death had been for the best. It was a nasty cliché, and anyway nobody knew for sure whether it was true. We had lunch. The sun shone on the trees in the cemetery and lit up the Virgins and crosses, but it no longer came into the house. The authorities called from Portland. Sara took the call and handled it well. We would head out there tonight, she told them in the end. Pablo called at about four to say he'd landed in La Guardia, and we told him not to bother coming home since all of us would be flying out from there at six thirty.

Sara told me that Michael O'Neal had called at about nine thirty in the morning and that when she'd told him the news he'd exclaimed "Yes! Yes!" twice, the way sports fans do when their team wins.

"Poor Michael," Sara remarked, and I didn't know whether she'd said because the boy was in so much pain or because she thought he was a little naïve.

We did everything. We even threw his ashes in the East River one sunny afternoon. When I was able to return to my work and looked at the painting again, I retouched the foam – which had been good, very good, too good – and today it's hanging up somewhere in Boston.

Time passed. The rest has not been silence, no. The silence will be here any minute now.

Thirty-Three

I asked Ángela to read me the last ten pages of these writings, and she had a hard time deciphering my handwriting. At this point I'm just guessing as I write, as my eyesight fades, so I've decided to stop and focus on looking at the world with the eyes of the spirit – to listen to music, which Ángela is going to have to learn to play on my computer, and listen to the tanagers. I think a lot about Jacobo, I think about Sara, I think about the two children I have left who come to spend time with me for a few days every year, about Venus, who comes with them too and reminds me so much of Sara at her age, and I feel warmth in my heart. Venus has two ten-year-old boys, identical twins, black, the best-behaved, gentlest, gangliest boys you can imagine.

I could dictate to a recorder and listen to what I've said, but I've grown tired of words. I'm going to write down the lines I wrote after a walk I took with Ángela along the colonial-era road near her house a year and a half ago. In them, I'm describing what I saw from when we set out to when we reached the banks of the Apulo River, which rushes tumbling down enormous rocks. I will write it in the form of a poem, more akin to a painting, as these were notes for a canvas that my eyes will no longer allow me to paint.

> . . . *On the left is a house where they've got macaws.*
> *Everywhere is the sound of the river.*
> *You reach a cobblestone road and go up it.*
> *In the valleys there are ferns;*
> *beyond the valleys, coffee plantations,*
> *and sometimes large boulders*
> *overgrown with pitayas.*
> *The wide road ends*
> *and the narrow one continues,*
> *skirting, to the right, bouldered meadows and,*
> *to the left,*
> *steep fields of coffee that sometimes look like thickets,*
> *dense brush.*
> *The sound of the river gets louder and louder.*
> *The road dips and reaches the wooden bridge,*
> *which, above the torrent, unites the green between the two slopes.*
> *This is the bottom. Each stone that hits the water,*

*and each of them, stone and water, flows together and forms that form
     that has no name,
  as it is there that words run out.*

Last night I sat for a long time in my chair on the porch. I went to fetch
a bottle of rum I keep in the kitchen and had a few swigs, not too many,
slowly, as I felt the darkness enter me, full of invisible stars. I am not sad
in my old age – quite the contrary – though it makes me melancholy to
think about Jacobo, to think about Sara. "When I'm hungry I eat, when
I'm thirsty I drink," say the Taoists. And I would say, "When I'm hungry
I eat, when I'm thirsty I drink, and when I'm sad I get melancholy."

My life up to now has been a good one. I experienced the other
side of pain, its opposite shore, and with oils and pigments I sometimes
thought I touched infinity. What more could a human being hope for?
It is possible that I have many years ahead of me yet and will live as long
as Antonia Latorre Estrada or Ellen Louise Wallace, but I will do that
without too many words, and it is possible that in that way I will come
to know new territories, other spheres.

I will always still have the big light, the light that has no boundar-
ies, that has no forms.

Breaking news: we've just learned that Ángela's ex-husband beat the
fern girl half to death. Ángela's son said he beat her so hard he split her
frenulum. I didn't even know she had a frenulum. He's in jail, of course,

charged with attempted homicide, and her brothers have threatened to kill him. Nobody believes they'll actually carry out their threat: they have a reputation for being all talk and no action. I'll have to look for a temporary gardener while we hire a lawyer and get him released. Assuming they don't kill him.

I asked Ángela to write the last of these pages. At first she refused because of her spelling. I remembered something she'd said once about towels and towls.

"Don't worry," I told her. "Honey is sweet whether it's spelled with an *o* or a *u*. Besides, I'm only going to dictate one word."

A word that has been handled too much, like love and so many others, and has lost its power.

"Well, sure, okay," Ángela said. "So which way do you spell honey, then?"

"You're awfully astute, aren't you? No matter what I say, you stay right on track."

"Awfully what?"

"Sharp, bright. Go on, then, go ahead and bring me the coffee, and then I'll dictate to you."

She came back. She picked up the pen. I dictated. She looked at me gravely.

"Here?" she asked. I had left a space amid what I am writing right at this moment, and I'd already inserted the punctuation.

139

"Here, where I put the exclamation point."

"Same size of handwriting?"

"What?"

"Same size of handwriting?"

"Yes, so I can see it."

"All right," she said, and wrote without hesitating:

Wunderful!

archipelago books
is a not-for-profit literary press devoted to
promoting cross-cultural exchange through innovative
classic and contemporary international literature
www.archipelagobooks.org